what belongs

what belongs

STORIES BY
F.B. André

RONSDALE PRESS

RONSDALE PRESS
3350 West 21st Avenue
Vancouver, B.C., Canada V6S 1G7
www.ronsdalepress.com

Typesetting: Julie Cochrane, in New Baskerville 11 pt on 15
Cover Design: Julie Cochrane
Cover Photo: "#20 Chinatown Wall" by Jules André-Brown
Author Photo: T. Brown
Paper: Ancient Forest Friendly Rolland "Enviro" — 100% post-consumer waste, totally chlorine-free and acid-free

Ronsdale Press wishes to thank the following for their support of its publishing program: the Canada Council for the Arts, the Government of Canada through the Book Publishing Industry Development Program (BPIDP), and the Province of British Columbia through the Book Publishing Tax Credit program and the British Columbia Arts Council.

Library and Archives Canada Cataloguing in Publication

André, F.B. (Frank Brian), 1955–
    What belongs: stories / F.B. André.

ISBN-13: 978-1-55380-044-6
ISBN-10: 1-55380-044-3

    1. Caribbean Area — Fiction. 2. Canada — Fiction. I. Title.

PS8551.N3592W43 2007   C813'.6   C2006-906327-3

At Ronsdale Press we are committed to protecting the environment. To this end we are working with Markets Initiative (www.oldgrowthfree.com) and printers to phase out our use of paper produced from ancient forests. This book is one step towards that goal.

Printed in Canada by Marquis Book Printing, Montreal

These stories are dedicated to
Franka, Debra, Renee, Roger and Mike
my sisters, my brother, and my other brother

ACKNOWLEDGEMENTS

I thank my family, Tricia, Jules and Carla,
whose love and support is my world. Special thanks to
Rachel Wyatt for being my first reader, and for suggesting
the wonderful title. Thanks also to Jay Ruzesky.

I cannot thank Ronald Hatch and Ronsdale Press enough.
Ron's patience and attention to every detail made this a
better book. Every writer should be so lucky.

CONTENTS

What Belongs

"We might even be kissing cousins," Merry Gibbs says in a wondering voice.

Henry Estes likes the sound of that; he likes the route her long legs take to get down to business with the ground, and he also likes what he sees coming *and* going as Merry agrees to try and sweet-talk her granddad into giving him more than the time of day.

Merry's granddad remains full of suspicion behind his living room curtains, checking up on Henry every few minutes but unwilling to step outside.

"Granddad is really the one you want to talk to," Merry says. "He's been around forever and a day. And he's full of stories about our family history."

Henry's enchantment with Merry gives way to another excitement: he may have found a living link. The rule of thumb is your grandfather's grandfather — that's how far back most of us can claim memories. Merry's granddad is well into his eighties, and that puts him in the ballpark.

Henry is a doctoral student in Afro-American studies; it would be too much to hope for, but this Mr. Gibbs might even be a direct descendant of Mifflin Wistar Gibbs — the key subject of his dissertation. While researching his subject, he came across an interesting sidebar: in 1858, Mifflin Gibbs led a delegation of thirty-five blacks from San Francisco to Victoria, "to evaluate the prospects of employment and settlement in the newly created territory of British Columbia."

The Governor, James Douglas, gave his personal assurance that the black settlers would be "granted all the same rights and protection as all other citizens." On the strength of this assurance, several hundred blacks left San Francisco determined to seize the opportunity.

Mifflin Wistar Gibbs was a resourceful entrepreneur who soon made a considerable fortune in the early gold rush days of British Columbia. Gibbs had great success as a merchant, contractor and property developer. He served as treasurer on the first Victoria city council; he helped negotiate the entry of the new province of British Columbia into the Canadian Confederation. Mifflin Gibbs lived in Victoria for more than a decade, and on his return to the United States he had several other successful careers: he became a lawyer and registrar of new lands; he was the first black to be appointed as a judge in Arkansas, and indeed U.S. history. Towards the end of his long and distinguished life, Mifflin Gibbs was accorded another honour; he was appointed to the diplomatic post of United States Consul to Madagascar.

Henry Estes' academic interest is spurred by a personal connection: he is from Oakland, and his ancestors were almost certainly among the settlers. His thesis is in part an attempt to retrace the route that Gibbs and the settlers took, his research has veered off into an inquiry: what became of the settlers? why are there so few footprints?

SCOTLAND, 1815

"When you sought my hand, you showed me only a sweet face and soft words, but now I see how truly stubborn a husband I am saddled with."

Jessie Hamilton's marriage to John Douglas is off to a rocky start. Her first task is to reacquaint her new husband with the manners and customs of his native Scotland.

"You cannot expect me to welcome your three bastards with open arms, and raise them in our very house, John Douglas?"

"I'll hear no such talk," John Douglas says. "These are my children, they will be treated as such, and raised in accordance with my wishes."

"Something has to be done." Jessie matches her new husband's wooden stare with practicality. "There is still some fair hope of acceptance for the two younger children, but the older boy shares your temper. He is sullen, and he is *dark*."

"James is a serious boy." John Douglas takes pride in his son. "He will not be a burden to you much longer, I've already made arrangements to send him away to Lanark for schooling."

Jessie is greatly relieved to hear this news. James is only twelve, and yet he is possessed of such a strong will that she greatly fears his influence on the two younger children, and indeed on his father.

"And after Lanark? What then?" Jessie will not admit to being a scheming sort of woman, but she feels the stir of new life in her womb, and she has already given some considerable thought to the protection of the interests of her future offspring.

"James will make his way in the world," John Douglas assures her. "His future holds as many possibilities as the sky holds stars; perhaps he will return to the Guianas and claim his birthright. Or perhaps he will make his way to a new frontier."

"At least speak to him about his surly manners," Jessie insists. Her husband has been away in the world, and perhaps he is right, perhaps there are places where bloodlines are of no consideration? But Scotland is not one of them. And Jessie resolves to do everything in her power to make sure that her unwanted stepson's destiny unfolds in some faraway land.

John Douglas sighs with exasperation; he has spent many long years away in the Guianas in pursuit of his family's sugar interests. He has neither patience nor the need for the approbation of society. But for the ready sake of harmony with his new bride, he will speak to James before he leaves for Lanark.

"I am sure that I will like Lanark even less than this house, Father," James says with quiet certainty.

"It's a foolish man who rushes to judgement without first taking the time to look for himself," John Douglas tempers his advice to his headstrong son.

"Why do they say that I am too dark?" James queries his father. "Why is the matter of the colour of my skin of any consequence to anyone?"

"Only fools judge a man by outward appearance," John Douglas replies, hearing the hurt and confusion in his son. "What you hold in your heart is the true measure of a man."

"They say that my mother was once a slave?" James reveals more of the hurtful insults. "They also say, that since you never married my mother, I am to be a bastard always and forever."

"Your mother was the freest woman that I have ever know in my life, and the most beautiful," John Douglas states with absolute conviction.

"You are like her," John Douglas gives his son courage to take with him to school at Lanark. "You are a Scot West Indian. You are a new sort of man, James. You are the best of both worlds."

VICTORIA, 2005

"You want to go to the Ross Bay cemetery?" Merry quizzes. "Do you always take your dates with you to such places?"

"Are we on a date?" Henry mocks surprise.

"We had better be on a date, mister." Merry sets him straight. "I didn't get all nice for nothing. You want some of my picnic lunch? You'd best bring out your best manners. I want doors opened, and please and thank you, Merry, every step of the way."

"I would never dream of treating you in any other way." Henry catches on quick, he hurries ahead to hold the door to his rental car open for her. What could be more perfect than going to see where the dead are buried with the most alive woman he has met in the longest forever?

"What exactly are we looking for?" Merry asks.

"Headstones," Henry Estes has not done much field research, but he has some textbook notions. "We want names, year of birth, year of death. I've been down to your provincial archives. I can't say they were helpful, and I will say that they were downright suspicious. I didn't present the right credentials. I got me some of that famous Canadian politeness. But I did manage to get a list of names.

"Several lists in fact. I got a list of newly registered voters. And I got a list of new citizens. Do you know that the militia — the first police force of Victoria — was composed entirely of blacks? 'The African Rifles.' They were a local attraction. People would turn out on Sunday afternoons to watch them do their drills. But I've yet to see one black face among your current police."

"Why would something like that even be a bother to you?" Merry wonders.

"Black and white don't go together, in Oakland, we keep to our own lanes." Henry's laughter doesn't cover his unease with this topic. Merry thinks it's way too early in the day to be so prickly, and she knows an easy way to change the subject.

"Tell me more about your Mr. Gibbs?" Merry asks.

"Mifflin Wistar Gibbs should be an American icon." Henry warms up fast when it comes to pitching his thesis topic. "His life had more twists and improbable turns, more rags-to-riches adventures than even Horatio Alger at his syrupy best could have penned. Gibbs was born in Philadelphia, in 1823. He was active in the Underground Railroad, and in the abolition movement. And he was a close friend of the famous orator, Frederick Douglass."

Henry hopes that all his scholarship is making a favourable impression on Merry, and her smile is all the encouragement Henry needs.

"In 1850, Gibbs moved out west to San Francisco. He was a skilled carpenter by then, but prejudice wouldn't allow him to practise that trade. He became a shoe shiner. That's how he made a start on his fortune, shining shoes for '49ers in front of the Union Hotel in San Francisco. Pretty soon he and his partner — Lester — owned an Emporium for fine boots and shoes, imported from as far away as Paris and London.

"There were plenty of opportunities in California back then, but it could all be taken away by force, or with the stoke of a pen. When a 'poll tax' was imposed on black businesses, Mifflin Gibbs refused to pay and his goods were confiscated for sale at a mock auction. He became a 'circuit rider' for equal justice, travelling up and down the state and organizing opposition to the 'Black Laws.' By the mid 1850s, Gibbs was publisher of the *Mirror of the Times*, an abolitionist newspaper. When the call went out for settlers in the new northern territory of British Columbia, Mifflin Gibbs led a delegation to check it out.

"Who sent out the call?" Merry asks.

"Turns out, it was the Governor himself," Henry says. "Now why would a Governor way up here in Victoria, extend an invitation to a group of blacks all the way down there in San Francisco?"

FORT ST. JAMES, 1825

"Do you favour your mother or your father?" James Douglas enquires.

"Am I Indian or Scottish?" Amelia Connolly correctly deduces his meaning. "I am neither." Amelia has given this very question some considerable thought. "Why sometimes I think I must be a new sort of person."

Her words confirm what James Douglas feels: he has found his match and mate.

"Tell me more about the Guianas," Amelia Connolly asks her new suitor. "This place of your birth. Where there is no such thing as winter?"

"It is true indeed." James Douglas has neither the gift nor the habit of small talk, but he will say anything if it will keep him in Amelia's good company. "There is only rain and sun. There are no other seasons. Day always gives way to night with alacrity, and there is very little twilight, or dawn, for that matter."

"How very strange." Amelia is very much taken with James, and she chooses her words in ways that encourage his tongue. James finds it easy to speak freely and naturally with her, and for once he is able to discard his serious mien.

William Connolly, the Chief Factor and Amelia's father, has also taken note of his young trader's determined interest in his daughter, but a match has already been made for her hand. He thinks he may have to reassign young Mr. Douglas, his best trader, to a new post. It is better to remove the fuel than fan the fire. Still, he will be fair and give him a listen. He will have one chance to make his best case for his daughter's hand.

James Douglas believes in forethought: that is the great lesson he has learned so far in his life. At school at Lanark, he learned to keep his mouth shut and listen first to the boastful folly of others. Soon he was able to pick out and pick apart their weaknesses. It is a stratagem that has served him well, and he has quickly become an astute trader. But he senses that he must now take an entirely different approach if he is to win the approval of the Chief Factor.

"Sir, your fair daughter Amelia, her mother is an Indian from these parts. Is this not so?" James Douglas begins to make his case with all earnestness.

"Yes, that is indeed so." The Chief Factor is puzzled by young Douglas's query.

"Sir, I have been called a 'Scot West Indian.' I am the offspring of a Scotsman such as yourself, and a free woman of colour. I submit to you, Sir, that your fair daughter Amelia is also a new breed of person. It is as if we are fashioned into new cloth. I see the evidence of this in the way our minds meet and conjoin. I call upon you to release her from her betrothal. Amelia and I, we are intended, and we are surely meant to be as one."

The Chief Factor is bemused, but if ambition is any measure, then this young trader, Mr. James Douglas, will be an able provider for his daughter. And perhaps there is even some merit to his argument: can a person who possesses the intermingled blood of two races have some natural advantages? It is hard not to be biased in favour of one's own flesh, and his Amelia has shown both resolve and a sweet disposition. James Douglas has come from far, and he will no doubt go even further. He is the better match. The Chief Factor soon comes round, and agrees to the marriage. But he also advises young Mr. Douglas to keep his theories on the superiority of mixed races to himself.

VICTORIA, 2005

"Turns out, your Governor, James Douglas, was passing for white," Henry Estes says. "There are quite a few references in the archives to him being 'dark,' and 'a mulatto.' He and his wife — who was half native — were both said to be 'sensitive' about their family backgrounds."

"I suppose all of that must have mattered way more, back then," Merry, who is of mixed racial heritage herself, allows. "Do you think it still does?"

"Is this where we turn?" Henry is not going to drive smack into that argument. A standing line of trees are at close attention, as if guarding the entrance to the Ross Bay Cemetery. The trees have grown taller than the purpose for which they were intended, and now shade and close off the cemetery from the adjoining residential neighbourhood; the ocean provides another natural boundary for the cemetery.

"There's more history in a cemetery like this than in the precious archives, if you know how to look," Henry says to impress his date. "Let's find the Douglas family crypt. And let's see who's buried next to and around and about the old Governor."

The Douglas family crypt is prominently marked, and Henry with a willing Merry for an assistant is soon taking notes of the names and departure dates of those interred nearby.

A righteous group of senior citizens are on a spot patrol of the cemetery. Headstone tipping and graffiti tagging are practically an epidemic, and these retirees have vigilance as their cause. It is also a pretty good excuse to get some fresh air. And they demand to know what business exactly are Merry and Henry up to?

"You folks are at the wrong cemetery," one of the seniors says with the blunt certainty that old age allows. "Blacks wouldn't be buried here. Ross Bay is for whites. The Jews have a tiny little strip of a thing, up near the top of Cedar Hill. If I were you, I'd try Harling Point — the Chinese cemetery."

"Is this cemetery still for whites only?" Henry sounds like a dog that wants to show off his bark and his bite. Merry hears Henry's annoyance, and perhaps it's all those trees closing in, but it does seem two shades cooler.

"The Chinese cemetery is much nicer," the senior citizen assures them. "It's very well kept up. When you get to my age, you'll take notice of such things."

"A picnic and a show. Now who could ask for anything more?" Henry's mood recovers as Merry unpacks the picnic. The parking lot of the Chinese cemetery is filled with a small circus: movie-making in progress. Henry and Merry have their picnic and watch the show. It is an exquisite sort of tedium: cameras and cables and lights have to be moved into place with extra sensitivity for those long buried below.

"They're digging up the past," Henry comments about the scene being shot.

"It's a bone ceremony," Merry says.

"Could be," Henry allows. And he thinks again how Merry is so full of surprises. "If it is, they're doing it all backwards. It looks like they're getting ready to bury something. They wouldn't be burying bones here? They'd be digging up the bones and sending them back to China someplace for reburial."

"That's where you're wrong," Merry says. "The point of the bone ceremony is to reunite your ancestors. These folks have been buried here long enough: this is home now."

Henry admits he hadn't thought of that, and they look for someone to ask. Merry's guess turns out to be exactly right. It's a documentary, not a movie, and someone else is wondering, like Henry, what has become of their ancestors.

Henry's thoughts are never far from his dissertation, and he cuts everything to fit the frame of his research. He returns to wondering about the black settlers. When does a place become home? When can you stake your claim? When does it become automatic? — "We are from here. We belong." Do you have to be born there? Do you have to work hard, fall in love, and raise a family? Or do you just have to die there?

It's closing in on a hundred and fifty years, but he expected something more in the public record. A church or a school, some notable achievements, even a juicy scandal or two? Several hundred men, women and a whole lot of children — where are they? Footprints, people always leave footprints.

"Are you disappointed?" Merry asks as they leave the Chinese cemetery.

"Not in the least." Henry has the luck and the common sense to say exactly the right thing. And Merry's smile makes Henry forget. Facts and arguments, names, dates, places, events, the invisible cloak of history — all the things that hold you in place — fall away, and now he is pulled along in a current of pure wonder.

FORT ST JAMES, 1829

"Amelia, that husband of yours can be so insufferable." John Connolly tells his daughter what she already knows. "When he was captured by Chief Kwah, I feared that his life would come to an end all too soon. The fact that he is still alive is a testament to his strong will and his skill at bargaining. He's my best trader, but at times he drives too hard a bargain on himself and others."

"James's intentions are always good and honourable." Amelia is quick to defend her husband.

"Why is James so harsh in his dealings with the Carrier Indians? And I am not the only one who holds to such an opinion. Mr. George Simpson, the Governor of Rupert's Land, has described James to me as 'furiously violent when aroused.' Is James intemperate with you in any manner, Amelia?" John Connolly is concerned for his daughter's very safety.

"No, Father, I can assure you that he is not." Amelia again hastens to her husband's defence. "James is sweet, and looks to my every care with gentle concern. But he believes that the Carriers — that all Indian peoples — can do more with their lives. James insists that Indians must be forced to learn the lessons of industriousness, and until they do, they are deserving of harsh treatment. I have tried to moderate his views," Amelia confesses, "but he is strong willed and holds firmly to his beliefs."

"His obdurate stance leaves me with little choice." John Connolly fears a disaster in the making. "It will sadden me greatly to lose your good company, Amelia, but I have obtained a transfer for him to Fort Vancouver. He will now serve under Mr. John McLoughlin, who is of good humour and even temper, and perhaps some of that will impress itself upon James. It will be a fresh start, he will have a clear path to advancement, and I have no doubt that he will be a Chief Factor within a decade."

"I am sure that you are right." Amelia agrees with her father's judgement, but she knows her husband's temper. "I will do my best to make James see this transfer as an opportunity and not a slight."

FORT VICTORIA, 1850

"I have met men like Richard Blanshard," James Douglas holds a low opinion of his rival, the newly appointed Governor. "He has come out here expecting to play the part of an English country gentleman; he is in for the rudest of surprises."

Amelia Douglas is proud of her husband, he has accomplished a great deal in a short span. James Douglas became a Chief Trader in 1835 and a Chief Factor in 1839. He personally selected the site for Fort Victoria on the southern tip of Vancouver Island in 1843. It was his stewardship that made Fort Victoria the main pacific depot for the trans-shipment of furs from the interior by 1849. And yet, when the time came to select the first Governor for the island, he was passed over. Amelia knows that her husband still smarts from the sting of this slight.

"Blanshard will not last a year," James Douglas predicts. "I will make certain of it. And I promise you, this slight will not be readily forgotten."

Amelia Douglas does not want any such promise from her husband. She agrees that he has been unjustly treated, but she urges him to turn away, suggesting that such a stratagem will be to his advantage.

"How so?" James Douglas is hot-tempered but far from foolish, and he has a great appreciation for his wife's shrewd counsel. No man could ask for or deserve a more stalwart companion than his Amelia.

"You are right about Mr. Blanshard." Amelia has her sources among his household help. "His resignation awaits only the acceptance of the British Crown. And he has complained both privately and publicly that you are the source of his despair. He has said that it is your intransigence with the striking miners and your harsh treatment of the local Indians that fuel fears of attack."

"Blanshard is soft and weak." James Douglas has only scorn. "You cannot tame a wild place such as this without a firm hand."

Amelia Douglas knows that her husband is sorely offended by the slight of being passed over for Governor. And she has heard the snickering whispers, that he is a half-breed, a mulatto. She has heard such slings and slurs all her life, too.

"England knows that you are the most able man but if you are to become Governor, you must hold your temper," Amelia pleads. "Let them see the man that I see. Show them the man who is fiercely proud of his children and who holds such high hopes for their futures. Show them the wisdom and compassion that a new breed of man is capable of."

VICTORIA, 2005

"Don't you tire him out," Merry warns. "Granddad gets confused real easy."

"Of course." Henry agrees with everything Merry says. It's the only way around her. Mr. Gibbs is his most promising lead, and his last chance to get some answers before he heads back to Oakland.

"If you want answers, you have to ask the right questions," Merry says. "The reason why men do what they do is always the same."

Now what does she mean by that? Henry hardly has time to wonder; Mr. Gibbs is ready to receive and volley.

"Merry tells me you're a history professor?" Mr. Mercier Gibbs has agreed to an interview, but he has his own list of questions. "Merry says you want to know about our family tree? I suppose you will want to start with my second cousin, Lance. He's the only truly famous one in the bunch. He played test cricket for the West Indies."

"You are not from Canada? From Victoria?" Henry asks, dismayed.

"I don't know what Merry told you," Mr. Gibbs says. "I've been here a long long time, but I was born and raised in Guyana. It used to be BG — British Guyana. But now is just Guyana. I came to Canada to further my schooling. I came to get a Master's degree in Education Foundations. I planned on going back to become a school principal. But I met a girl in Winnipeg, and the next thing I know, I have grandchildren who think they are so smart, smarter than me."

Henry listens half-heartedly now to Mr. Gibbs' account of his childhood at play on the banks of a river that emptied into an ocean a world apart. He is picturing a big chunk of his research breaking off, like an iceberg, and melting into this vast and distant sea.

"Tell Henry about grandma." Merry brings out some of her famous sun tea, and that smile of hers might as well be a spell conjured from pure sunlight.

"My Maria, she was my sunshine, for fifty-seven years." Mr. Gibbs lights up at the very memory of his wife. "I met my Maria at university in Winnipeg, but she was from Victoria, born and bred. Her family came out here when the place first opened for business. She was an Alexander."

Henry Estes is at full attention now; Mifflin Gibbs married a Maria Alexander. After he came up to Canada and scouted things out, Gibbs made a trip back to the States to marry her.

"Funny thing," Mr. Gibbs chuckles at some ancient joke, "my mother-in-law used to say that there were Gibbs in the family tree already. And she didn't want to shake too hard and find out that we were related. And it was remotely possible."

"How so?" Henry Estes tries to contain his surprise. It is important not to lead or to contaminate a source.

"You're a history professor? You must know that after the American Civil War there was a Back to Africa movement," Mr. Gibbs explains. "As usual, those things were organized with high hopes and small wallets. When the money ran short the government looked for repatriation solutions closer at hand. Land grants were purchased on the British islands of Jamaica, Trinidad, Tobago, Grenada, and also on the mainland in Guyana.

"Now my understanding is based more on family gossip than gospel," Mr. Gibbs qualifies, "but apparently, it was a long-ago relative of mine who recommended Guyana for settlement. And that is why to this very day there are so many Gibbs in Guyana."

Henry Estes is familiar with this history; it intersects with his thesis subject: in his long and interesting life, Mifflin Gibbs played a significant role in the post Civil War period of reconstruction. His proposals usually centred on education. His solutions to the problems facing the black man always featured self reliance through enterprise. And he was also a strong proponent of repatriation and resettlement.

"My Maria," Mr. Gibbs embarks on another reverie, "she was named after her grandmother. Did I tell you how her family settled out here from the get-go?"

Henry waits for Mr. Gibbs to continue with his story, but he has fallen silent.

"Do you know anything at all about the Estes family?" Henry prompts. "I believe they also settled around here? Or perhaps over on Salt Spring Island?"

Henry's questions come a little too late; Mr. Mercier Gibbs is a ship that has sailed, you can wave all you want, but he has turned to face another horizon.

FORT VICTORIA, 1858

Mifflin Gibbs hides his fear better than most. He learned how as a fatherless boy. He was just eight when his minister father died and left his invalid mother with prayer as her only recourse. He has been away in the world ever since, and at thirty-five, he can rightly claim to have had more bold adventures than most men will ever encounter in a lifetime.

When the delegation set sail from San Francisco to Fort Victoria, their dismay was palpable; the *Commodore* was overflowing with miners, men of the very sort that they were seeking an escape from, men who made no pretence of tolerance, and took every turn and malicious delight in disadvantaging the black settlers. Will Victoria be some sort of cruel hoax or trap?

The *Commodore* arrived in Victoria on Sunday, April 25, 1858, at noon, just as the locals were streaming out of church. The stir of curiosity among the locals at the sight of a delegation of thirty-five Blacks, was lost in the general alarum of four hundred and fifty miners disembarking, and suddenly whispers and rumours are confirmed in one bold shout — Gold! The Rush is on.

It hardly seems worth noting in all the bedlam and delirium, that the Governor of the new territory came down to the harbour to greet the delegation personally. Mr. Mifflin Gibbs acted as spokesperson for the delegation, and he was considerably cheered by his first impression of the Governor and his wife.

"He is a man of strong character," Gibbs reports to the delegation, "and in truth, I am equally impressed by his wife, Mrs. Amelia Douglas. She holds more than a fair sway in her husband's affairs, I'd venture to guess. And she has extended to me a most gracious invitation, I will dine with them this very evening."

The delegation is greatly concerned with the sincerity of the Governor's offer, and they instruct Gibbs to take care in determining why the Governor has extended a direct invitation to them? To the coloured? To settle these new lands?

"This Governor is newly minted, but he is no stranger to these parts." Mifflin Gibbs is an astute judge of opportunity and character, and he has already gleaned some pertinent information from his initial meeting. "The Governor wants settlers who are not so fixed in their loyalty to the American Eagle. He wants to know if we are willing to serve the British Lion? If we are granted the same rights and freedoms as all other settlers, I will say to him, good Sir, we are indeed willing to become King George's men."

"Are you married? Mr. Gibbs?" Mrs. Amelia Douglas inquires.

"Sadly, no." Mr. Gibbs hesitates to confide in someone whom he has just met, but his hostess, Mrs. Douglas, has a disarming manner. "There is someone whom I would very much like to ask. She is a woman of great beauty, charm and high education, why she is a graduate of Oberlin College, a much distinguished school."

"Why are you so reticent? Mr. Gibbs." Mrs. Douglas has an insistence about her. "A woman with so many attributes will not wait too long for any man."

"Madam, you have just given voice to my greatest fear," Mr. Gibbs ruefully responds. "No man should undertake so serious a matter as marriage, without good prospects. And in all good candour, I cannot imagine how I can be deserving of such a sweet creature."

"Mr. Gibbs, you will not know what you are deserving of, if you do not ask." Mrs. Douglas has a practicality that goes along with her persistent character.

"Good Sir," Mr. Gibbs turns to Mr. Douglas, "I must congratulate you. You are truly blessed with a wife who is possessed of a genuine heart and much good sense."

The Governor has said little over the course of the meal; he is a man of serious mien, who gives the appearance of woodenness, but now he seems ready at last to voice his opinion.

"My Amelia is indeed a woman of sterling character." The Governor turns to his wife and says with a sweet tenderness that surprises Gibbs, "The best and boldest thing that I have ever done, was to seek your hand, my dear."

Mrs. Amelia Douglas's response is a smile of such radiance that Mifflin Gibbs' first impression of the place Mrs. Douglas holds in her husband's esteem is confirmed. He feels a strange sort of envy for this man who holds his love so precious and close, and he resolves to speed his return to Ohio to seek the hand of his one true love, Miss Maria Alexander.

"Sir, three hundred good men are awaiting word in San Francisco, they are eager and ready to bring their families and take up the challenge." Mifflin Gibbs decides to boldly state his case. "They need only your assurance that they will be treated as men, and they will come willingly."

"Where are your people from?" the Governor asks.

"They are from all over," Gibbs explains. "Some are free born men, and some others have sought an escape from the yoke of slavery, but they are all men in search of a better destiny."

"I have heard reports that there are a great many children born out of wedlock among you. Is this true?" the Governor asks.

"Many of the children are indeed born out of wedlock," Gibbs confirms.

"I have also heard that a great many of these children are the offspring of two races?" the Governor enquires.

"That is correct, Sir." Gibbs can make no guess as to the intent of the Governor's question, but he adds a heartfelt plea. "It is a fact that these children are oftentimes the unfortunate byproducts of forcible unions between whites and blacks, but they are no less deserving of a better future."

The Governor resumes his wooden silence, and the dinner concludes. Mr. Mifflin Gibbs still has no assurance from the Governor. He looks to Mrs. Douglas for some sign of encouragement, but she is now engaged in household matters. He has not journeyed this far to leave without an answer, and he is determined to press the point.

"Good Sir —"

"Mr. Gibbs," the Governor interrupts his earnest plea, "you should make all haste. Go and bring your people from San Francisco. You have my assurance; they will have all the same rights and freedoms as other settlers.

"This is a new age," the Governor proclaims, as if it were a fact beyond all refute. "And this new age needs a new breed of men."

Mifflin Gibbs and his delegation returned to San Francisco with the news of promise and opportunity. There was a new Jerusalem to the north, and three hundred men along with their wives and children were willing to answer the call. It was decided to purchase a herd of cattle and the men would go on ahead by wagon train. The women and children would journey by ship; the *Brother Jonathan* was chartered for this purpose.

Gibbs would rejoin them later; first he made all haste to Ohio to seek the hand of his beloved, Miss Maria Alexander. She succumbed to his ardent entreaties, and they soon embarked on a lengthy honeymoon, back to his native Philadelphia, before settling in Victoria, some several months later.

The men drove the herd of cattle up through Oregon, bringing the necessary supplies to start a new life. But they met with delay, and when the *Brother Jonathan* sailed into Victoria with its most precious cargo of five hundred women and children, there was no one to greet them, save the wife of the Governor.

"The Governor very much wanted to be here to welcome you in person, but he is away, fighting the sort of battles that men always seem to need to fight." Mrs. Amelia Douglas apologizes for her husband's absence.

The children, released from the confines of the ship, are eager to frolic, and their mothers call out for stern order.

"Let them play freely; it would indeed be easier to stop the wind," Mrs. Douglas says.

"What would you like to do first?" Mrs. Douglas tries her utmost best to put the women at ease.

The women settlers say that they would first like to give thanks to the Lord for their safe passage. Mrs. Douglas readily agrees to their request and she leads them in prayer. The women are thankful for all the kindness shown by Mrs. Douglas, and quite naturally they seek her advice. Where is the best district for them to settle? Is there a church where they could worship in peace? What about schooling for the children?

Mrs. Douglas is careful to hear their concerns, and she gives every assurance that her beliefs are also shared by her husband.

"When my husband became Governor, his first official act was to request funds for two schools. All children who want to learn will have that opportunity. If you worship the same God, then you will most assuredly be welcome in His house. And as for a district to settle? I would favour no one place above the other. I urge you to spread yourselves out everywhere instead. When there are no distinctions, when you can walk freely about, no one can claim or deny, what belongs to us all."

VICTORIA, 2005

"It's a long way to come to die," Henry comments.

"They've come back to spawn too," Merry points out.

Merry is giving Henry the grand tour; they've been out to Goldstream Park, where the salmon return from their epic journey. And now they are off to the Observatory, a favourite spot from Merry's childhood.

"It looks like a golf ball that's landed on an anthill," Henry teases. He is in no hurry to go up to the Observatory. If this feeling would last, he would take residence in this one bubble of a moment forever.

"It doesn't look like much from down here," Merry agrees, "but once you reach the top, you'll get a good idea of the lay of the land and what it must have looked like, way back before when."

What does it take to find your place in the universe? Henry returns to wondering about the settlers and the missing branches of his family tree.

"Why did your Mr. Gibbs go back?" Merry asks.

"He was homesick," Henry says. "He even said so in his autobiography, *Shadow and Light*."

"My granddad would say that you're 'book stubborn.'" Merry hasn't decided if she's looking for a flat-out argument, but Henry had better not be thinking that he can just up and leave without saying *something*.

"Your Mr. Gibbs came to Victoria, he made his fortune, he lived in the best part of town, he got himself elected to city council. He pretty much had the run of the place, and then he went back because he was homesick?"

"Why else?" Henry says.

"Where did he go when he went back?" Merry asks.

"He went to Oberlin College," Henry supplied. "He went to study law."

"Oberlin College? His wife's alma mater," Merry says. "He went back because of his wife."

"It's far more likely that Gibbs left when Douglas was no longer the Governor." Henry puts forward another hypothesis. "Gibbs and Douglas were both shrewd customers. Gibbs did pretty well in his business dealings with the government; he started up the Queen Charlotte Island Anthracite Coal Company, and he won several contracts even though he didn't always have the lowest bid. Maybe Gibbs no longer had an entrée to high society when Douglas stepped down? And maybe the black community no longer felt like they had a benefactor in high office?"

"Try and imagine what it was like for her?" Merry asks Henry to consider. "Mrs. Gibbs would have been by far the most educated woman in these parts back then. Do you think she had any chance to exercise her brains or talents? She left way more behind in the States than he did. When it came time to raise her family she went back home, and your Mr. Gibbs went with her. And maybe that accounts for some of what all happened to the hundreds of settlers?"

"You're applying modern sentiment on past thinking." Henry is still talking as if he's in an academic discussion. "Victoria was more of a starting point. Some settlers could have become homesick, but it's more likely the settlers dispersed by simply chasing after the gold, scrambling to get in on the next big strike."

Merry is not interested in reason over passion. What more can she do to get this sweet and stubborn fool to look through the past to the present? Merry points out an old abandoned farmhouse from one of the very first settlers; it's nestled in a low valley, like a dropped stitch on a furrowed quilt. The road follows what was once a walking trail, then a wagon path.

"So much of history is paved over," Henry observes.

"Henry? Do you think it so impossibly strange that a man would make such a move for love?" Merry searches Henry's eyes. Henry meets and holds her gaze.

"When I first saw you working away in your garden," Henry says, "I knew I'd better find the nerve."

"This is where we turn, Henry." Merry smiles sweetly at him. The road twists and climbs to the Observatory, and they both know that the way ahead is full of sweet surprise.

What the Future Holds

Erica Kim is naked and standing on her head. She is doing so on the advice of her neighbour Cheryl, whom she babysits for. Cheryl has four kids, and Erica has to respect her neighbour's opinions on fertility. Cheryl told Erica to do a headstand after intercourse to give the little swimmers a better chance. It's a proven fact, and she even saw it in a movie. Erica's mother-in-law has also e-mailed instructions for a certain exercise: right after intercourse, Erica must lie flat on her back with her legs pointed straight up against the wall, she has to tighten, hold and relax the muscles in her pelvis while doubling the number two, four, eight, sixteen . . . Erica gets as high as eight thousand one hundred and ninety-two before she loses count.

Wilson Kim, Erica's husband, is a graduate student from Korea. He is already dressed, and playing with a borrowed rifle. He admires the heft of it, the way it feels when he carries it low. And now he hoists the rifle to the jamb of his shoulder and sweeps the room; he stops when he has his wife in his sights.

"Wish me luck," Wilson says. "When you e-mail my mother, ask her how to make her venison soup. Yes?"

Erica wriggles her toes at him. She is not sure how many times she is supposed to repeat this exercise, but she abandons it when she feels the urge to pee. Cheryl and her mother-in-law both recommend against peeing; Erica is supposed to hold off on peeing for as long as she can.

Wilson waits by the door. He is like an eager child who is ready to go outside and play, and when he leaves a blast of cold air fills their townhouse. Erica does a neat half somersault. She thinks about a hot bath and decides against it; she is not sure if that will help or hurt her chances. Erica is trying to beat the clock, to get pregnant and have her baby born before her husband completes his graduate studies in Canada. She has been trying for one year and seven months now; her husband still thinks that he can complete his studies in two and a half years. She would like to give her baby the gift of birthright: to grow up knowing that there is always the possibility of a door that opens out onto a new life. The door has shrunk to a window.

In the student housing complex where they live, she can see the playground from her kitchen window; it is full of colourful bouncing, bouncing balls, lottery winners all. Erica recognizes some of the children by their bright hockey sweaters and ski jackets. She earns a little money and a lot of gratitude from babysitting, by holding down the fort for a few hours. She comes early to decorate the common room for birthday parties and she stays to clean up at the very end. We don't know what we would do without you, they say. Erica is thanked and she is appreciated, but Erica does not feel as though she belongs. She is missing the winning ticket, and there can be no true admission without it.

There might still be some fertile time left in her ovulation cycle, but Wilson was so eager and pleased to be going on a deer hunting trip with his colleagues that there was no way she could insist; perhaps this time — perhaps the cells are already dividing, two, four, eight, sixteen . . . Erica suddenly feels light-hearted, and she has four whole days to herself.

⌒

Len would have preferred to live further out, but his wife said they had to think ahead, about a school for the kids, down the road. The subdivision was fairly new and it backed onto the freeway; the university had just built a student housing complex on the edge of its endowment lands, which backed onto the subdivision. There would be lots of young children from all over; there was a co-op daycare right in the school, and it was a Block Parent community.

We have to get involved, his wife said. When they had kids, they'd be over at the community centre all the time. They both loved to skate, and the community centre was building an out-door rink to go along with the basketball and tennis courts; his wife signed both of them up.

Len works in construction, and the job of looking after the ice at the community centre became his right from the start. At the first cold snap he goes over to get things started. Several people are out walking their dogs, and Len thinks again how there are fewer kids and more dogs in the neighbourhood now, and if it weren't for the university student housing complex, the elementary school would be in trouble. The community centre is really feeling the pinch. Programs are being cut left and right; you need kids to make it all work.

They tried and tried. They went to see specialists. Their reproductive lives were placed in the hands of others: her eggs and his sperm were passed around and around in so much frozen hope until Len could no longer stand it. He wanted to smash all of their samples and specimens, and unplug them from all of the gadgets and procedures that promised to unlock every secret in the universe.

They took a holiday to a place called St. Maarten, in the Caribbean; someone from work told his wife that it was the most romantic place in the world, and who knows? maybe even a little magic, something special, could happen?

Len said the way he saw it, they had two choices: they could stop trying or they could start over. He knew how much she wanted kids, and if she wanted to leave him and try with someone else, he would understand. Len thought he was being noble. Don't be such an idiot, his wife said. Nothing can change the way I feel for you. It was the worst day and the best day in Len's life.

They looked into adoption, they talked about it, they went to an agency, but they could no longer stand the idea of expectancy. It went on the back burner, and then on the shelf. After a while, neither one of them brought it up. The neighbourhood began to change; families moved in, families moved out. A new mall went up on the other side of the freeway. There was talk about building a junior secondary but that went nowhere. The new mall provided the tax base, and everything new went up on that side of the freeway, which was just as well. They had a pet cat for a while, but it ran away. They put up posters all over the neighbourhood, but no one had seen it. Perhaps it had made it across the freeway and started a new life.

⁓

"What sort of underwear does Wilson wear?" Cheryl asks. "It could be something obvious, you know, like switching from briefs to boxers."

Erica sips her tea. She is not going to discuss her husband's preference in underwear with her neighbour.

"Making babies has surprisingly little to do with the mechanics of sex." Cheryl has taken courses, she has read up on gender differences. "It's all about ovulation and sperm motility. You guys should go and see a specialist."

Erica agrees. Erica is very good at agreeing; she has mastered that essential art. A wife does not always have to agree with her husband, her mother-in-law has said, countless times, but she must always obey, if there is to be harmony. Erica agrees with that too.

"Sperm counts are dropping like mad all over the world."

Cheryl shares this bit of information. "There are certain foods that Wilson can eat to boost his count. It could be as easy as broccoli. Maybe you guys eat too much spicy food?" Cheryl has another thought. "That kimchi stuff is lethal. I've seen how Wilson eats it like candy."

"If kimchi prevented babies," Erica rejects this argument, "there would be no one born in Korea."

Cheryl laughs. Erica is always so literal. It must be something cultural. Cheryl's youngest gets into a screaming match with himself. Another one of her kids interrupts with a complaint about the other two. Cheryl yells: a mother's blanket injunction to stop whatever it is that you all can't share!

"I'd kill for a little quiet time. Enjoy it while you can." Cheryl clucks with envy. "Come over for supper?" Cheryl is an insistent mother hen.

"Thank you, but I am quite fine," Erica declines.

Erica walks Cheryl's four kids to school. The youngest is three and in pre-school; he is quite capable of walking but Erica pushes him in a stroller so they can all keep up. He hates being pushed. He is not a baby; he yells at Erica, go faster. His class is at eight forty-five, and he has to be picked up at ten-fifteen. If the weather is good, Erica waits at the school playground.

The school playground is a giant sandbox full of swings and slides, a scaled-down obstacle course with more bouncing balls. Erica waits with her empty stroller. She is on nodding terms with some of these mothers of newborns and toddlers. They speak a kind of English that is outside Erica's range, but she can decode the piping babies. They make a music that tugs, that calls to something urgent in Erica.

Next to the school playground is a baseball diamond that overlaps with a soccer field, and beyond that — a community centre. Erica includes the centre on her walking circuit. Today it is cold enough for the outdoor rink to be flooded, and Erica goes over to watch how the ice is made.

"You don't want to stand there." Len points at her with the nozzle of a hose. "The wind," Len explains, "will carry the spray right to where you are."

Len is trying to take the kinks out of the hose, but every time he flexes, it coils back into its sleeping snake shape. Erica studies the problem of the hose and sees the solution. She goes to where it begins to coil and lifts it up; Len is now able to spool it out.

"Good thinking," Len says. He points for Erica to continue lifting, and he walks the kinks out.

"If I show you where, can you turn it on? Wait until I say go. Okay?" Len hurries to the nozzle end and gives the signal. The hose jumps into life.

"Come and see how it's done," Len invites. "The first thing to check on is the wind." He shows Erica where to stand. "You do not want to be outside working with a high pressure hose when it's windy."

Len directs the powerful stream to the rounded corners of the rink. The water is already finding places to pool.

"A high pressure hose is all right when it comes to flooding a rink, but not for making good skating ice," Len explains. "Outdoor ice is a totally different proposition from indoor arena ice. You have to let the water find its level, and then you have to go back over it and fill in the uneven patches. Do it right and you can get weeks out of an outdoor rink; do it wrong — do it over."

Erica nods. She understands the importance of doing the little things right.

"Do you live in student housing?" Len asks. "You can skate for free here, if you live there. That's a pretty good deal."

"I cannot skate," Erica states. "I would like to learn how. But I am afraid to fall."

"You could take lessons," Len suggests. "What size are your feet?" Len studies Erica's boots. "I bet you're no more than a five? There's a bunch of old skates inside; I bet we can find something to fit you?"

"I have to go soon." Erica is feeling a little self-conscious now.

"There's nothing wrong with the skates," Len says. "They're still good; the kids outgrow them real quick. You have small feet, I bet we can find you a real good pair."

"That's quite okay," Erica says.

"It will only take a minute." Len hands the hose over to Erica. "Don't wave it about too much," he says. "Keep it steady."

The force of the water surprises Erica; it's a job for two hands, and she tries to make slow steady passes as Len has been doing. It's work that feels like play. At the far end of the rink she can already see the ice forming, like the milky skin on an omelette. The recess bell rings and the kids come streaming out. Erica has to go. The man has not returned; Erica holds onto the hose for as long as she can. She tries placing the hose gently down, but it jumps about like a thing alive, and as Erica runs away from it she gets a good soaking.

Len is carrying a box of skates, and he calls after her to wait, stop. Erica hurries across the baseball field. The children are being picked up and her child is searching the playground and he can't find her. He begins to cry. His voice is a bleat that makes Erica's heart skip, and she races towards him in her wet clothes, pushing her empty stroller, and suddenly feeling so very foolish.

Wilson is a Hotmail husband. More and more couples are meeting like that these days. It is not so strange anymore. There have been many successful matches made in this way. It takes the pressure off. First you chat, and then you exchange pictures. If there is no spark, it is much easier to say goodbye in a chat room. And if there are hard feelings, you can block the sender, or close your Hotmail account and get a new one.

There is a danger. You can never really be sure exactly who you are talking to in a chat room. Erica is now quite sure that someone else did the talking for Wilson. And that someone is his mother. Her mother-in-law's e-mails have a familiarity to them, a way of saying things that Erica used to find so endearing, but now she feels that Wilson has cheated — as if he got the answers without studying for the test.

"You do not want to be stale cake on the shelf," Wilson's mother said when the match was being made. "Wilson must marry before he goes away to study. And you are already twenty-six, so you better hurry." Wilson's mother was absolutely positive; her son was a good catch.

It was the prospect of going away that tipped the scale in Wilson's favour. Erica's parents also had a suitor in mind; he worked in the same office as her father. He was a widower, seventeen years older than Erica, and he already had two young children. But Erica did not want this ready-made family. She did not want to be a nanny; she wanted children of her own. And she saw herself projected, as his nursemaid and then his widow, still young, but too old ever to find someone else.

"Have you done your exercises? It takes more than romance to make a baby." Wilson's mother has several more suggestions, positions for them to try. Erica hates answering e-mail from her mother-in-law; it's like replying to a conversation that is already over. Wilson's mother knows all about his hunting trip, and she has already sent some recipes for venison soup. Her mother-in-law has also sent a revised list of Wilson's favourite foods, and "more ways to keep his energy up."

Erica thinks about taking that hot bath. The swimmers have had their chance; now it is up to nature. Erica draws a hot bath. She studies her naked body in the bathroom mirror, looking for any signs of change. Cheryl said that she knew right away, except for her last one. The last one snuck by, but three times out of four is not bad. Erica has heard other mothers say the same thing, that they just knew. How early is too early? And how soon before she can take the pregnancy test? She should know these things by now, but every month hope takes a different shape.

Erica slides down into the tub and tries to visualize the life forming inside of her. First it is a spark, and then a cluster of cells that won't divide. She can never quite picture herself and Wilson with a baby. Wilson is very traditional; Erica fully understands what her mother-in-law means by this now. Wilson is used to having every little thing done for him, and he sees absolutely no reason why this should change. Erica's hope is tiny. Perhaps when Wilson becomes a father, he will no longer be so much of a son?

Erica can hear more than the plumbing on the other side of the thin townhouse wall she shares with Cheryl: squeals of laughter spill out from the pipes; more often it is a sharp scream, followed by a stream of crying and Cheryl shouting I told you so. She hears Cheryl and her husband argue — the same old argument about money and time, and never having enough of either. Sometimes she hears them making love and trying to be quiet about it and failing happily. Cheryl has offered a blanket apology. The walls of student housing are built thin on purpose, so you don't get too comfortable, so you can't wait to move out. Erica insists on pretending that she cannot hear a thing. That way she does not have to admit to envy and longing for a house full of such noise.

It takes a moment for Erica to realize that the noisy pounding is at her front door. And now she can hear Cheryl calling and calling her name. She climbs out of the tub, twists a towel around her head and puts on her bathrobe. Cheryl and her husband are both at the door, and Erica is startled to see that the someone else with them is a policeman.

The policeman takes off his cap and holds it in front of him like a shield, as if he is protecting his heart. Cheryl, who knows everything to know about being a mother, puts her arms around Erica, and leads her to the sofa. The policeman stands. There's been an accident. The policeman has been trained to make eye contact and to deliver his message in a calm and level manner. Erica refuses to meet the policeman's look. She wants to leave a space for doubt.

Wilson is hurt, but not too seriously, the policeman assures her. Cheryl thanks God. Erica stares at the blank wall. She is already wondering what she will say to Wilson's mother. At the door, Cheryl's husband gets more details from the policeman. Black ice. Loose gravel. It happens every hunting season. What can you say — people think, people don't think.

"They're looking into an airlift," Cheryl's husband reports back.

All four of Cheryl's kids come in a disobedient spill into Erica's living room; they are like alarms going off. Cheryl yells for her husband to take them home, all the while hugging them so very close.

"Come home with us. You shouldn't be alone at a time like this," Cheryl insists.

"No, I am quite fine, thank you," Erica says. She may go for a walk later, and she will be sure to drop by. What she wants now is a moment to herself.

"Of course." Cheryl understands, she is a mother.

When Erica stands up to walk Cheryl to the door, the fabric of the couch sticks to her legs and her bathrobe comes undone. She is naked, exposed. Erica quickly tugs her bathrobe tight about her, cradling her belly, and protecting what she now knows for sure is growing inside.

⌒

After supper, Len goes back to finish the rink. He hopes that the cold snap will last for at least a week; it's not so much that he begrudges the time it takes to get the rink up and ready from scratch, but the fact is, once you have your base sheet down, it's simply a matter of upkeep. And it's better to do it at night. It's colder. And you don't have all the eager beavers waiting to jump on and start carving up the ice before it has a chance to set.

First, Len scrapes the surface with a snow shovel in large over-lapping ovals, then he compacts the shavings into the corners, or uses them to patch up any obvious weak spots. It would be great if he had steam. With steam you'd get some melting action, and also quicker refreezing, which makes for a better surface. Len has to settle for hot tap water; he can do the entire rink in twenty-five minutes. Sixteen minutes is his best time.

Fresh ice is his reward for doing all the work, and Len always goes for a skate afterwards. He likes the greedy expansive feeling of being the only one at the rink. When they first moved into the neighbourhood his wife used to come skating with him all the time. She took lessons as a kid, and she could do all the fancy stuff. She could really fly. They'd skate together for awhile, but he knew he held her back. He'd stop and let her go at it. Len loved watching her skate, and she used to put on quite a show, just for him. Then his wife stopped skating; she gave it up. It was too much of a risk, back in one of those years when they were still wishing and trying.

His wife did everything she could think of to get ready to be a mom: she read up, she cut out and filed away articles for future reference, she went to baby showers and paid close attention to each and every newborn, she learned the shuffle step — the one you use to quiet a crying colicky baby, she even mastered the one-hand diaper change. Len took a hands off wait-and-see approach; fatherhood was a bridge he would cross only when he came right smack up to it. His wife never brings it up, but every once in a while when Len thinks about it, he always comes out at the same place. How can you lose what you never had? And the thought passes quickly, like a stray cat, like a wish not granted on a shooting star.

Len should have turned off the lights. It's best not to give out the idea that the rink is still open. The rink used to stay open late, but it got way too rowdy. People from the other side of the freeway would come over and take advantage; it's always the same few hooligans, but they spoil it for everyone. Someone is approaching from the school playground — the Asian woman from earlier today. Len is not good at guessing which country they're from. Some people can tell right off, but he can't. The woman watches him skate, and Len does another lap before he circles over to the boards where she's standing.

"I can still get you a pair of skates?" Len offers. The woman doesn't say anything. Her eyes are watery from the cold, and she is shivering like something crazy. Now what the heck is she thinking? Len wonders as the silence grows like a shadow across the ice.

"Come on." Len decides that it must be some cultural thing about asking. "We'll get you all set up. And I'll throw in a quick skating lesson."

Erica obediently follows Len.

"Let's see if I guessed right," Len says. "You're a five. You have to lace them up tight. Tighter than you think." Len shows her how.

Erica tries on the skates. She looks down at the sparkle of new ice on asphalt, and it makes her think of diamonds, and how diamonds come from coal. When the policeman stood before her, in that moment of not knowing, Erica didn't wish for Wilson to be dead, but she was surely hoping for a release from her present life. She has no idea what she will say to Wilson's mother or how she will say goodbye to Wilson. No one can know what the future holds, and for now Erica has decided not to be afraid. She has the sudden hope that her child will have all the things that she does not.

When Erica tries to stand, her skates give right out from under her, and she gives a small scream of surprise.

"That happens to everybody." Len catches and steadies her.

Erica begins with small steps; she stumbles every time. She has no choice but to hold on to Len.

"It's okay." Len leads her out on to the ice. "Take a minute, get your balance. I'm not going to let you fall. You can hold on for as long as you like."

A Love like Water

When Mrs. Kalicharan flew out to Vancouver to stop the marriage, her intention was to swoop down on her son Anton, grab him by the scruff of his neck and shake some sense into his head. But now Anton is in a tangle of tubes, fluids draining in and out of him, kept alive on electricity, and by her prayers.

"Did Anton ever have trouble with headaches?"

Mrs. Kalicharan's hearing is fine-tuned to the apparatus that is keeping her son in limbo, but she can still hear the warning bell.

"Is there any history of seizures?" the official asks.

Mrs. Kalicharan is a short woman. She fishes for her shoes under her son's bed. She wants every inch as she arches her back. Mother scorpion hisses. The questions retreat but they will come back later. Mrs. Kalicharan returns to her son's bedside.

Anton was always sickly. The rest of her children grew like weeds. The usual childhood diseases barely slowed them down. Measles, whooping cough were done and gone in days; broken bones healed in two-twos. Anton didn't even start school properly until he was seven, and he missed so much time that no one realized he was bright until his older brother Rodney, who was always hard-headed, started suddenly to receive good grades on his assignments, grades that he couldn't recreate in the classroom.

A suspicious teacher looked beyond disbelief and found a prodigy. Great things were predicted; as soon as Anton was old enough, he could pick and choose his scholarship. His seizures started with puberty. Anton and his mother were the only two people in all of Guyana who didn't think that spelled an end to his plans. They looked for the right combination of doctoring and bush medicine. They devised a regime. Anton took daily supplements of the popular remedy "Beef Iron & Wine." Chinese bitter melon and shining-bush tea were also incorporated into his diet. Twice a week he went for a rub down from a bones-and-sprains man to keep him aligned.

When Anton's claim for a scholarship was denied on medical grounds, it was Mrs. Kalicharan who refused to take the no. She searched until they found a doctor who would allow hope. Various tests were performed until a set of results was produced that could be taken as confirmation of his fitness, and Anton was granted his scholarship. She had hoped that Anton would have had the good sense to work at his studies and keep his tail quiet, but somehow he managed to get himself tangled up in a two-car accident. A hit and run. Anton was badly injured and the occupants of the other car fled the scene. What the official asking the questions was trying to determine was who was at fault.

As she keeps her vigil at Anton's bedside, Mrs. Kalicharan has some questions herself, Boy, who sent you to play man? What were you doing driving car? And why do you think you're ready for marriage? All she can do now is pray, and she suspects that her prayers and his student health insurance might not be enough.

"Komar was always the lucky one," Roop's wife boasts loudly into the phone. "Komar has already found a good girl for Tahal. When Nadira comes home from work she will help me send the e-mail pictures. You will see for yourself."

Roop is lifting weights in an exercise room he's set up off the kitchen. Since his retirement he has increased the intensity of his daily workouts to keep in shape. His wife is in the kitchen with the phone locked into the cradle made by her ear and shoulder. She stands close to the docking station, not trusting the magic of wireless phones. One hand stirs a pot of cardamom tea, and the other fishes through her purse for her deck of long distance calling cards. She will be on the phone for hours, and the news of their grandson's marriage will be trumpeted far and wide.

"Komar says the girl is very satisfactory, considering. There is a big shortage of girls in India these days. I'm telling you, it was our bad luck to be born at the wrong time."

His wife cackles to her friend. Roop is not going to listen to what else his wife's brother Komar, has to say. He decides to cut his reps short and go for his walk now.

"— Roop! Roop!" He hears her hollering and he hurries down the steps before she can catch him with a list of urgent things that he must do. The wedding, now item number one, will take over their lives and cost him a lot of money. There will be at least one trip to India, and his wife will meddle and make countless plans. The wedding will consume her. That is his one and only consolation from this sad and sorry business.

His sixteen-year-old grandson, Tahal, stole a car to go joyriding with his friends. The car belonged to the uncle of a classmate who was out of the country, but Tahal and his friends knew exactly where the key was kept. Then while they were joyriding, a car smashed into them. Or so they said. And instead of staying to face the music they scattered like cockroaches. The driver of the other car was badly hurt, and the problems multiplied from there: stealing a car, failure to remain at the scene and driving without a license. All of these charges will be small potatoes if the other driver dies.

So far, the police have not caught Tahal and his friends. But Tahal was the one behind the wheel, and at sixteen he would have to face trial as an adult. The courts will be looking to set an example. All of these were reasons why Tahal was sent packing off to India. And now this hurry-curry marriage before the boy even has a chance to grow his first beard. It is not right. But his word carries no weight in his own house.

He is already at the corner. Look left, look right, look left again. Now cross. That is how he was taught, and that is what he tried to teach his son and grandson. His son, Jamal, never learned to stop, look and listen. When Jamal was in high school he got a girl pregnant. It takes two his wife said, and then she reminded him that they were even younger than Jamal when they had their first one. She was always quick to defend Jamal. His wife was also eager for a grandchild. They took the child in, and when Jamal and the girl broke up, they continued to care for Tahal.

When Tahal was a boy, Roop recalls, he used to walk him to the elementary school. At this time of the day the road is not so busy, but in the mornings you have to watch sharp for your chance. Once you get safely across, the rest of the way is straightforward. First, the road continues through the middle of a cemetery, then there are a few more blocks and another main road to cross just before the school, but there is a cross-walk with a light there.

At fourteen Tahal started to show signs of bad behaviour. Like father, like son, Roop reflected. At that point he had insisted that the boy spend some time with an Imam. One or two afternoons a week, a few hours on Saturday, it was not too much to expect. The boy needed something to ground him; he needed to understand his religion, his history too.

Tahal didn't like wearing his *patka* and he was always misplacing his under-turban. When the Imam suggested it was time for Tahal to begin tying his *pagri*, the boy found all sorts of reasons to avoid it.

"Don't rush him," his wife warned. "You will make him turn his back on God."

"Birds attack me all the time," Tahal complained. "It's because of the turban."

"What fresh nonsense is that? A man wears his turban with pride." Roop insisted that his grandson show respect.

"Come and see for yourself," Tahal challenged.

He went with his grandson along the road to the cemetery. And as soon as the crows saw them approaching they began making a vociferous racket, swooping down, cak-cawing and clawing at their turbans. Apparently the birds nested in the trees at the very place where Tahal always waited for his friends to gather on the way to school. In the winter the birds did not see him as a threat, but now it was spring and nesting season. Tahal was the interloper; the crows were quite rightly protecting their young.

＞

"He's definitely improving, don't you think?" Linda, Anton's fiancée, whispers. She has just arrived for her shift at Anton's bedside, having dragged along her roommate Winnie for a shield against Mrs. Kalicharan. On the other side of the bed, Mrs. Kalicharan gives the two of them her best withering glare, but she is relieved to have a break and silently leaves.

Linda moves closer to Anton's bedside. She has incorporated the shock of his accident into her daily routine, and now she is building future scenarios: it will be touch and go but he pulls through, then there is a fade to a tender rehab sequence and a dissolve into a brightly lit future.

"You said yes, but you haven't said I do. You'd be crazy to go ahead." Winnie is working from a different script.

"Stop it!" Linda does not want to resume this argument. Not here. Not at Anton's bedside. What if he can hear?

"Look at him," says Winnie pointing to Anton in his tangle of tubes. "Are you good at gardening?"

"How can you even say such a horrible thing?" Linda is appalled. There are some things you don't even think about, and if you do, you never ever say them out aloud.

"Ant, Ant," Linda calls, resuming her vigil. "I'm right here, Ant. It took me only twenty minutes. The traffic wasn't as bad as usual. I've got a parking pass now. Somebody from the Knights of Columbus arranged it for me."

Linda has a line she holds on to. She has been told that Anton may be able to hear her, and that news of the familiar could help reel him back. She repeats the details of her day in excruciating detail.

"Ant, Ant. I had egg salad for lunch."

Winnie cannot stand to listen to any more of it and heads to the cafeteria. She will look for something sweet to bring back as an offering, but she will not apologize or ask Linda for forgiveness. Their friendship is based on convenience; together they can afford a much nicer apartment, closer to work. And they share similar tastes in men. Winnie saw Anton first, but she didn't want to date him because he is a student in the faculty where she works. She passed on him, and then changed her mind.

When Winnie wrestles with her conscience it is usually a no-contest, a few sumo seconds that ends with all of her doubts being pushed clear out of the ring. But this time she's caught in her own headlock. The first time with Anton she can defend. She could make a case. Linda and Anton weren't officially dating yet. So it wasn't really cheating. And after he and Linda got engaged, it was always one last-time sex, which is the hardest kind to stop. Besides, Linda and Anton are only getting married so that Anton can get his immigration papers. If she had told Linda right away, it probably wouldn't even have caused much of a row. Linda would have accused her of being a greedy, selfish bitch who had to have everything for herself, and Winnie would have agreed, one hundred percent. They would've compared notes on how he was in bed, and it would have turned into a giggle, eventually.

Anton has to take some blame too. It takes two to tango. And now it's all a big mess. Does she have an obligation to tell her? Especially now? What sort of friend would she be if she let Linda go ahead with the marriage? Isn't it better to give her a good reason to break it off? But on second thought, Linda probably wouldn't even believe her.

⁓

"Anton was driving your car. How come?" Mrs. Kalicharan cuts into line next to Winnie.

"I never use it during the day," Winnie says, defensively. Anton's mom is so intense she creeps her out. Winnie knows that she is dealing with someone who is way more determined than she will ever be.

"What sort of work you does do?" Mrs. Kalicharan demands.

"I'm a program coordinator," Winnie replies. "I work in the same faculty where Anton is a student."

"Secretarial work?" Mrs. Kalicharan makes sure.

"Yes, I suppose so," Winnie replies.

"Why would Anton call out in his sleep for you?" Mrs. Kalicharan asks.

"He did? It could be that the last thing before the crash had something to do with me," Winnie answers quickly. "He could have been thinking, 'Oh no! I just smashed Winnie's car.'"

Mrs. Kalicharan is impressed by Winnie's quick thinking. If she had to choose between the two for her Anton, she would pick this one. The other one is too soft. Anton will need a firm hand.

"How could you let him drive? That is pure negligence." Mrs. Kalicharan can't help it. She needs to blame someone. "He's not supposed to drive; he's never even had a license."

"How was I supposed to know that?" Winnie's feathers are up too.

"We can't let the insurance people know." Mrs. Kalicharan is looking for a co-conspirator. "If push comes to shove, I can get him a license."

Winnie is not sure of the significance of this but feels as if she has just been enlisted.

"Which one of you know Anton first?" Mrs. Kalicharan asks. And again Winnie is not certain what the question portends.

"Anton was always pestering me for more lab time." Winnie recalls their first meetings. "He never stops until you give in."

"When that boy sets his mind, it's hard to say no to him." Mrs. Kalicharan loses her composure, and goes from sniffling to sobbing. Winnie is left to pick up both trays and follow Mrs. Kalicharan to a table in a corner of the cafeteria.

"I have some pictures of Anton I want you to see." Mrs. Kalicharan has made a career out of looking out for her son. Since this is the girl who owns the car, her instincts say that she could be a useful ally.

Roop's wife never liked living so close to the cemetery. She didn't like walking through the cemetery, disturbing the dead of others. They are not our dead, Roop had said. They had bought the house for a very good price.

There were very few brown faces in the neighbourhood when they first moved in. Still, Jamal managed to find the only Muslim girl his age, and get her pregnant, bringing shame down on both families. By the time Jamal's son Tahal was in high school, there were several Muslim boys his age, enough so he had a circle of friends.

There is a lot of new construction around the cemetery now and it is always dusty and noisy, Roop thinks. He watches a small procession as it enters the cemetery, the hearse moving at a measured speed. This driver understands; the dead are not to be hurried. The headlights and the emergency lights on the cars and the hearse are flashing in silent tribute. Last light before eternal darkness. The procession makes right-angled turns until they reach the burial plot. A few wreaths have been delivered ahead of time and are arranged on easels of differing heights. They make a frame with the mound of fresh earth around the open shadow on the ground.

Outlive your enemies but not your children, that is the way a life should end. Roop is a bystander, a respectful distance away, under the same trees where the crows used to attack Tahal. Since it is not nesting season, the crows ignore him, but they are also eyeing the funeral. They will wait to see if the leftovers are of any interest.

Every day since his retirement Roop goes for a walk. And every afternoon his walk takes him through the cemetery to the school grounds. Some afternoons he hears singing from a rehearsal or a performance inside the school. In the autoshop building down at the end of the laneway some boys are tuning up an old car. The tennis courts are often busy. He recognizes a group of boys who come regularly to play ball hockey. And sometimes a boy walks past bouncing a basketball on the exact spot where a murder happened.

A few years ago a boy was killed at the same high school that Jamal and Tahal attended. Jomar Lanot was playing pickup basketball after school when a group of boys attacked him. When he tried to run away, he was caught and beaten to death on the school grounds.

Jomar Lanot was a Filipino. Some of the boys who attacked him were Muslim. They were only a few years older than his grandson, the sons and grandsons of people he knew. It was a horrible and senseless crime. There was much talk about race and youth violence, and experts of all stripes offered opinions. There was enough blame and not enough responsibility. It seemed no one knew how to apologize. Everyone agreed that as the city grew bigger more innocence would be lost.

The blows that killed Jomar Lanot have been absorbed. One boy has been sentenced, and charges have been stayed against others. On a wall outside the school there is a plaque. Every so often in the news there is talk about building a memorial park. Roop looks for signs but the work still has not started. He often wonders about the family of Jomar Lanot and what they hold on to? He must speak to the family of the boy Tahal's actions have harmed. He must apologize in some way. He already knows his wife's opinion — "Stay out of it, Roop!" — but he will go to the hospital.

Linda has exhausted all the small details of her day, and now she has only one big thing left to say to Anton. She is late. It would be easy enough to take the pregnancy test and confirm, but in another corner of her mind where she makes her bargains with God, she is only allowed to hope for one thing at a time.

"Ant, Ant. Why won't you wake up? Please wake up. I need to talk to you. Ant, the doctors say that the worst is over; they think you're going to be okay." She studies his face. She thinks she knows for sure when he's dreaming; his eyes move rapidly and his breathing becomes shallow and very fast. Mrs. Kalicharan swears that she has heard him speak, that her Anton knows she is there, and he has called out for her. Linda listens intently to the steady hum of the machines monitoring him, the drip-drop of his IV, but she can attach no meaning to any of his noises.

Anton's actions are what won her over. He could be so silly and sweet. The first time he slept over, he insisted on making her breakfast in bed the next morning. He went through an entire dozen eggs before he was satisfied that he had poached the perfect one for her.

Linda searches her memory for more scenes like that. What she finds instead are doubts. After the accident she went to his room to tidy it up before his mother arrived. She found panties in his dirty laundry. They were most definitely not hers. Why would panties be in his laundry? What sort of woman leaves her panties behind? She decided to ask Winnie.

"He must have lent his room to a friend." Winnie offered a perfectly reasonable explanation. "When would he have had the time? He's at our place all the time. You two were practically glued together."

When she went to Anton's room, what troubled her even more

than finding the panties was what was missing. Anton is a student. He lives in one room. But he has so few possessions. Some students have photos or silly little things that they have brought with them to remind them of home. Anton's room had nothing like that. Other students are immersed in their work, their research, textbooks and papers. Anton's room had none of that sort of clutter; he does all his work at the lab. His room is a blank. He is a blank.

Before meeting Anton, Linda had already decided that she was tired of kissing frogs and hoping for a prince. She had grown weary of waiting on love. And then Anton arrived, and love found her. She knew why Anton wanted to get married, but she didn't care. In fact, she was the one who suggested speeding things up to avoid any problems with his student visa expiring. People get married for all sorts of reasons. Besides, she recalls reading somewhere that in most of the world it's all arranged for you. People learn to love each other. They must. She will put her trust in love. If she and Anton are meant to be, it will all work out. If she is going to have a baby, his baby, our baby . . . she needs a sign.

But all she hears is Mrs. Kalicharan and Winnie returning. Mrs. Kalicharan has stopped at the nurses station to give revised instructions.

Anton makes a gurgling sound. Linda comes closer. He's definitely trying to speak. He's coming out of it. Ant. Wake up. We need to talk.

"Ant? Do you love me?" Linda asks in a whisper.

⁓

When Roop checked at the information desk they assumed his brown face meant he was family and he was given directions to Anton Kalicharan's room. The only information that he has about the boy is from the news. Anton Kalicharan is a foreign student from Guyana. The only thing Roop knows about that country is from cricket. Guyana is on the mainland of South America, but it is a part of the West Indies for cricketing purposes.

There is more than one patient in the room. And there are other visitors. He hadn't expected that. And in truth he didn't really have a plan. He had hoped to summon the right thing to say, but now he is at a loss for words. Roop takes a few tentative steps towards the only brown faces in the room. Roop is relieved and grateful to see that the patient is awake.

Mrs. Kalicharan is at Anton's bedside, holding her son's hand. On the other side of the bed stands a girl. Roop stops, realizing he has attracted the vigilant eye of Mrs. Kalicharan. He begins looking around the room, then takes out a scrap of paper and pretends to read.

"Wrong floor, sorry," Roop says to Mrs. Kalicharan's face full of suspicion.

"Your boy, he is going to be all right? I hope so. I apologize." Roop nods and backs away.

Mrs. Kalicharan resumes stroking her son's hand. "Boy, you gave us so much worry."

"What were you dreaming about?" Winnie is on the other side of his bed.

"I was dreaming about you, Winnie. I had the craziest dreams."

"I bet," Winnie says. "They've got you on some pretty strong drugs."

"Where's Linda?" Anton asks.

"That girl has been by your side day and night," Mrs. Kalicharan gives Linda credit. "This one too."

"I thought Linda was here," Anton says.

"Linda was here when you started coming out of it," Winnie says. "She's really upset. When you first awoke, you were yelling my name. 'Winnie! Winnie! I love you!' I told her it was just the drugs talking, but she didn't believe me. She's pretty upset. I think she knows about us."

"Where did you learn such behaviour, boy?" his mother scolds. "Don't ever play the fool with love."

"You said you love me, Anton," Winnie murmurs. "Do you? Are you going to take it back now?"

Anton smiles and closes his eyes.

⌒

Roop feels like a bit of an ass, but he is relieved at the way it went. Perhaps he should take his wife's advice and look for a part time job. He retired too young. Lifting weights and exercising are not enough; he needs something more to keep busy. He could get a job as a security guard. He knows several people in that line of work. It would get him out of the house and the extra money would help pay for the trip to India for Tahal's wedding.

They should have more lights in this parkade at night, he thinks. If you can't see your hand in front of your face, how can you expect to find your car? Do not leave any valuables behind, he repeats the words on the sign. Remember your level. That is always good advice.

"Who's there?" Roop is sure he's heard a noise. He listens closely. Someone is crying, in pain. He is wary but moves towards the sound.

Linda is sitting on the ground between two cars. She is holding a broken radio antenna and she is bleeding from between her legs. Roop pries the antenna away from her.

"Why do such a thing?" Roop is horrified.

"You need help." Roop looks around, but the parkade is deserted. "Can you stand?"

Linda remains doubled over from the pain.

"I'm going to carry you, okay." Roop squats beside her. He slides his arms under her.

"Don't," Linda says. "You'll get blood all over you."

"Never mind about that. There's blood on my hands already." Roop lifts her easily. She is lighter than he expected. "Put your arms around my neck and hold on."

Roop begins walking quickly towards the elevator. Linda tightens her grip around his neck and pulls herself closer to his ear.

"Tell me what you know about love," Linda whispers.

"What? I don't understand," Roop says.

"What do you think love is?"

"I don't know."

"You must know something," Linda insists.

Roop remembers something that he heard, or perhaps it was something that he once felt.

"I think love is like water," Roop says. "No matter how hard the stone, water can cut through it. Water will always find a passage."

Linda clings to him. She is willing to believe in a love like water. She will put her faith in water now.

Old Pirates

I put off making the obligatory visit to my great aunt Vere for almost a month. After the first week, she sent word that I was expected for tea. By the second week I started to get phone calls from my mother in Canada. Why was I trying my best to shame her? How come I hadn't shown my face yet at Auntie Vere's? Go, and check up on her health, please.

Auntie Vere is in her eighties. She lives in the respectable part of Woodbrook, in Port of Spain. Her stately house dates back to the nineteenth century, and is the frequent subject of tourist photographs and postcard sketches. When I arrive at her house in time for Sunday tea, Auntie Vere has another visitor. A Mr. Boone, who stops to talk to me in the yard on his way out.

Mr. Boone's face and arms are sun-baked — a deep cured pink, like a ham. He has a random series of impressive moles, and his hair is cut so short it's like a dusting of salt and pepper, which makes it difficult to guess his age, but I would say that he is a well-broiled sixty.

"Call me Boots." Mr. Boone explains his nickname is from sports, cricket, football, and especially rugby. "When I put my foot into it," he steps into a demonstration of his famous drop kick, "I used to get incredible hang-time."

Boots is Auntie Vere's solicitor. His accent is British, but all his idioms are Trinidadian. "How you come to be family with Vere and Russell?" Boots checks my pedigree.

"On my mother's side," I reply. "Vere is my great aunt."

"Russell was one of my first clients." Boots establishes his link to my family. "I used to dream of owning a big house like this. Vere used to give music recitals; it was an extraordinary thing, man. Vere could make sweet music too bad, yes.

"Your daddy was in the oil?" Boots is trying to place me. "Shell or Texaco?"

"We lived in Point Fortin," I say.

"You wouldn't recognize Point Fortin now," Boots says. "The government went and buy out everybody." Boots has witnessed countless acts of bureaucratic interference. "And now they turn around and privatizing like mad," he adds. We nod and shake hands in vigorous agreement. Boots takes his leave.

"What did he say to you, boy?" Auntie Vere asks sharply.

"We talked about Point Fortin," I reply.

"Point?" Auntie Vere is irate. "Mr. Boone wants to hand me off to some junior piss-ant. I never met a more ungrateful man. Poor Russell must be spinning like top in his grave today."

It seems that Mr. Boone's crime is that he wants to retire.

"Don't fret up yourself like that, Miss Vere," Maxine says, as she enters the room. "Save your strength, you think I want for people to say how is Maxine who let you run down yourself?" Maxine consoles and cajoles all in one breath. I can't believe she still works for Auntie Vere.

"Come boy." Auntie Vere allows Maxine to steady and steer her into the sitting room. "Come and tell me how you get to be so much big shot that you can't come to see your old auntie up till now?"

Auntie Vere is not satisfied with the updates I give of my branch of the family tree. She insists on going all the way to the roots.

"You've never met my Richard?" Auntie Vere questions me closely about her son, who left Trinidad long before I was born.

"I've heard Mom and Dad talk about him of course," I say. "He's the famous one?"

"I don't know about that." Auntie Vere looks around her sitting room as if trying to remember where she put something of vital importance.

"Richard had a very nice career going in England." Auntie Vere locates her photo album. "I don't know why he even went to the States.

"This is my Richard." Auntie Vere flips through her photo album. "And this is his wife, Denise." Auntie Vere checks my reaction to see what I know, or think I know. It is an open family secret that Richard is gay.

"Is she from Trinidad too?" I decide to admit to nothing.

"No," Auntie Vere points, "she's a Filipino."

The woman in the picture has the broad smile of a bride on her wedding day, and the handsome man beside her is Richard. He is quite a bit older, and his smile is a thin line. The album is full of press clippings and publicity photos of Auntie Vere's almost famous son, Richard. He had some early success as an actor. For a season or two he even appeared on a popular daytime soap.

"I suppose," Auntie Vere says, "that all of this is before your time?"

Before my time, but not out of range of family gossip. When her son Richard finally convinced himself that it was not his misfortune or lack of talent, but simply that his look was out of favour,

he turned to the other side of the camera. Richard is now a pro-
ducer and director of infomercials, for "life affirming products."
Marriage is good for business; his wife is the on-camera hostess in
his productions.

"Maxine? Maxine?" Auntie Vere calls out. "That girl is so slow."

Auntie Vere is the only person on the planet in a position to
call Maxine a girl. Maxine started working for Auntie Vere when
she was seventeen, more than forty years ago. Her continued
employment with Auntie Vere is a constant source of embarrass-
ment for her children, who have — all praise and thanks to the
Lord — done well for themselves.

Maxine enters with a tea tray piled high with treats. Maxine
loves to bake, and she gets too few opportunities to show off.

"Don't forget to take a little something out for the driver,"
Auntie Vere says.

Maxine sniffs, she is insulted. How could Auntie Vere even think
that she would ever forget her manners like that?

"I made toolum and sugar-cake just for you, boy." Maxine insists
that I try a piece of each.

"The toolum is still my favourite," I say. Maxine smiles. Some of
the very best memories from my childhood have that exact same
smile in them.

"You still chasing those pirates, boy?" Maxine asks, about my
favourite game from childhood. Auntie Vere laughs at the memory with her.

"You see any?" I share this old joke with them.

We lived in Point Fortin, near the south-western tip of the
island, and a visit to Auntie Vere had the added excitement of a
trip to the big city. Auntie Vere's sitting room is filled with the
same suite of Danish furniture that she bought when teak was all
the rage. She resembles her Danish furniture. She is long-boned,
and her skin is blond-brown like teak.

From the sitting room, I can see into her music practice room.
A piano fills one corner, and it is covered with a hand-embroi-
dered cloth. Her cello is in its case, and is belly up to the piano.

"Do you still play?" I ask.

"I does give a few lessons, here and there." Auntie Vere absent-ly massages her hands. "But play? I can't really and truly say that anymore."

A conversation with Auntie Vere now is like folding time. When she goes into a story you never know where she is going to come out. Auntie Vere is almost famous in her own right, as a classical musician. She had gone to further her studies in England, but it was during the war, and her choice of music was out of favour.

"I always liked the German composers," Auntie Vere confesses, recalling her time in England. "And once I met up with my Rus-sell, he was in a big hurry and I was just glad to come back home from that damp, damp place." Auntie Vere was accomplished on the piano but the cello was her forte. What she missed out on by living in Trinidad was the opportunity to play at the highest level. Still, she had her brush with musical fame after her husband died. By the sort of accident that does occur regularly in a small place like Trinidad, she met a world famous conductor who was recu-perating from an illness. He invited her to record, and she went with him to New York for a time. He died, and the recordings that she made with him "are still tied up in the wrangling over his estate."

And so it went for the rest of the afternoon, until my tea is all gone, thank you, no. And I really don't have room for even one more piece of Maxine's delicious baking.

"Maxine!" Auntie Vere calls out. "Boy, get her to wrap some-thing up for you to take."

I've done my duty, which was more pleasure than chore, and now the next step is for me to make a full report to my mother.

"I hear from your mother," Auntie Vere says, her curiosity catch-ing back up to her, "that you have a big shot work?"

"I don't know about that," I copy her reply. "So far, all I have is a big title."

"You have to always be on the look-out, boy." Auntie Vere's stage whisper sounds like a warning. "This place is still full of old pirates, yes."

I look for Maxine to say goodbye; she is having her own high tea with my driver. Maxine has turned the old servants' quarters behind Auntie Vere's house into her private domain. The servants' quarters is about the size of a large garage, and is joined by shared plumbing to a laundry shed.

My driver's name is Selwyn Roberts. He has been chauffeuring me around for nearly a month now with impressive indifference. Roberts wears a uniform of his own contrivance: a Greek fisherman's cap, a white short-sleeve shirt, with a crest of St. George and the dragon on his breast pocket, and dark olive khaki pants. This is the first time I've seen him without his fisherman's cap, and it changes his features. He is nearly bald, which I guessed, but I have to revise his age, from mid-forties, to say, early fifties.

"Selwyn thought you was a Yankee, boy," Maxine clucks at me. "Why you didn't tell him you is one of we?"

Am I? One of we. I've lived more of my life away from Trinidad than in it. I am out of tune with the rhythms and the daily happenings — the keys that let you in on a place.

"How is Auntie Vere?" I ask Maxine. Her opinion will headline my report.

"She all right, steady on the main. But she have her troubles too." Maxine gives her frank assessment. "It have days when her bones does hurt her too bad. I try everything I know to try. Stinging nettle. Shining bush tea. Prayers is the only thing left."

I will relay this information to my mother, and she will get in touch with her cousins, who will *tête-à-tête* with Richard, and plans will be made for Auntie Vere to come up and see a specialist. And for the rest of my stay, I will be expected to file detailed reports on her condition to people whom I hardly know, and some — like her son Richard — whom I've never met.

"Wait, wait." Maxine hurries off to her kitchen. "I have some shortbread for you."

I work for a company that specializes in corporate takeovers. I can make better sense of my job if I think of it in terms of piracy. We raid ships, we capture and place them under our flag, we seize their cargo, and then we break the rest up for scrap. After a take-over, I'm sent in to offer assurance, to talk about restructuring and creating synergy, but what I'm really looking for is buried treasure, to see if there is anything left to plunder. I have a driver and a car, lodging at a Guest Hotel — which is a style of bed and breakfast with complimentary fawning, and an endless round of meetings full of intrigues, which I am the subject of but not a party to.

I didn't set out to conceal the fact that I was born in Trinidad. My family moved to Canada when I was fifteen. I don't have a Trinidadian accent anymore, yet my brother, who is only three years older, still sounds as if he never left. I can put on the accent, but it makes me feel foolish and self-conscious. I wouldn't want someone like Roberts to think I was mocking him in that annoy-ing "right mon" way.

I don't know if it is because Roberts now knows that I "is one of we," or because he also suspects that I am nearing the end of my stay, but he operates at a different speed. He is indiscriminate in the use of his horn, and he overtakes with zealous disdain. Roberts has also opened up the trunk of his life to me.

Roberts has a wife, who left him. When he went to prison. "What?" I say to Roberts as quietly as I can, and yet still be clearly heard. "What did you go to prison for?"

"Assault," Roberts says. "I don't think I should just give she the divorce, just so."

"How long were you married?" I ask. "Before you went to prison, and how long were you in prison?"

"That is a good question." Roberts drives on. "I was married for nine years and change, before I went inside. And I was in for nine years too."

"What kind of assault nets you nine years?"

"Oh, the other fellow died in hospital," Roberts replies. "And I got moved up to manslaughter. If I had had the money, I could've got off clean," Roberts swears. "All I had to do was call for a new trial on the grounds of hospital negligence, show reasonable doubt, and boom — ask for dismissal on jury mis-sentencing."

I have a pretty clear idea of how Roberts spent his time in prison.

"She," Roberts is adamant, "she could have helped me out. She could have done more to get me out."

Once you find out that someone is capable of the sort of violence that results in extensive prison time, it's hard to look at him in the same way.

We are on our way to Point Fortin to visit my childhood home, and Roberts has a request. He wants "to make a stop-off in San Fernando" to see his wife.

"My wife, she does live in Canada, too." Roberts fidgets with his fisherman's cap as he establishes his line of reasoning. "Is not only the divorce she come down to see about. Is we son, Carlton. He get his tail in some trouble. He get deported."

Roberts has put me in an awkward position. I have no desire to be involved in his domestic situation, but I much prefer this Roberts, who treats me like "one of we," to the indifferent Roberts, and I agree to accommodate his request.

The reunion takes place in the gallery of a house in San Fernando. Every so often, someone comes and stands in the doorway to make an exclamation point out of their displeasure. Roberts' time in prison has made him an outcast among his wife's family. And his son's present troubles are viewed as a direct reflection of him.

I understand why Roberts wants me here — I am a kind of witness to the fact that he has a steady job, and also a ready excuse. It is a strained sort of occasion, and Mrs. Roberts is dressed for it: she wears a skirt and blouse with a jacket and hat combination that would work equally well at a wedding or a funeral. I leave the gallery and opt to wait by the car. Someone remembers their manners, and sends a cold drink of juice out to me with Carlton, Roberts' son.

Carlton is the image of Roberts; he is not too far out of his teens.

He is wiry in the places where his father is now thickset, and his hairline is already on the same high retreat. In a slow and formal manner Roberts and his wife descend from the gallery. On the landing they exchange a few more words, and she gives him a big manila envelope. This completes the hand-over.

"You ready?" Roberts asks in a general way as he puts his son's things in the trunk. His wife goes down to the gate to watch for traffic as he reverses out of the yard.

"You must look out for one another," Roberts' wife says. She reaches through the window and touches her son on the cheek. Roberts and Carlton stare straight ahead. By the time we get to the corner and up to speed, full separation is achieved.

"We could make Point on another day?" I offer Roberts an early out.

"No, no, Chief," Roberts quickly replies. "Is good for a man to go back and see where he come out from."

"You remember Point?" Roberts asks his son. "I used to take you down there. You remember the beach at Cedros? We went to swim down there a good few times."

Carlton gives no sign of remembrance or response.

"Chief? Didn't you used to live in Toronto?" Roberts tries to engage me in small talk, to wring some words out of his son.

"Yes, when we first went up," I say. But nothing that Roberts or I have to say can draw Carlton out. He stares straight ahead, and the drive to Point continues in an uncomfortable silence.

My father worked for Shell, and then Texaco. The oil companies set up camps — gated communities — near their operations, where it was possible for expatriate workers and a few locals to live apart and within, "on an island on an island." We were always told how lucky we were, mainly because we had easy access to imported goods. When my father went to work for Texaco, we moved to San Fernando from Point. We didn't live in San Fernando for long. What I remember most about our time in San Fernando was getting ready to leave. My father went on ahead, my brother had his driver's license, and we still had the use of my father's car. We went back and forth to Point, holding on to our old life, but then the excitement of leaving took over.

As we come into Point I get the jump of recognition you feel from a once familiar place. Point Fortin was and still is little more than an oil company's camp. But it has a long history: it is where expeditions in search of El Dorado stopped to replenish supplies, and ships from Columbus on, came to get pitch for caulking from the nearby La Brea tar pits. The contours of the landscape still agree with my memories, especially along the shoreline. It is full of my childhood imaginings. Once I actually found some treasure: a piece of silver, rubbed smooth by the sea, but still shiny enough to conjure up pirates, who lay in wait in the coves along this coast.

Cedros is one of those coves. I take a walk in one direction to give Roberts and his son a chance. This used to be one of the nicest beaches, but all the offshore drilling has a price — the sand along the tide line is tinged with black, and the rapid stench of decaying marine life is mixed with the antiseptic smell of tar. I used to *break buisse* — sneak out of school and come down here. Strange things would sometimes wash up along the beach — the tangled-beyond-recognition carcass of an animal, person or thing. It's only a few miles to the mainland, across the Gulf of Paria to the mouth of the Orinoco. At night on several occasions, I saw a rowboat, and I heard the desperate and bold whispers of someone planning to escape with the tide and the moonlight into a new life across the Gulf in Venezuela. I didn't have any great expectations for and about my return to Point. But I did have a small epiphany of sorts — when you return to a place, after such a long time, there is more of a feeling of absence, than of ever being present.

"Where you get that *tampi*, boy?" Roberts is in no position to lecture his son about his misdeeds, but that doesn't stop him from passing comment.

Carlton smokes his marijuana out in the open; his eyes are red with defiance.

"If is more trouble you want," Roberts assures Carlton, "it have plenty right here in Trinidad, too."

I don't know the circumstances surrounding Carlton's deportation, but I agree with Roberts' line of reasoning. "You learned your wickedness in Canada, you should take your punishment in Canada." It seems cruel and unjust for Canada to send someone like Carlton back to Trinidad. He went to Canada at an even younger age than I did. What does he know about Trinidad?

Carlton has nothing to offer in reply; he is staring across the Gulf at the horizon. Roberts takes off his cap and his shoes, and strips down to his jockey shorts. Now he dares Carlton and me to do the same. We are the only ones on the beach, but I feel self-conscious. And I think Carlton does too. We watch as Roberts wades into the warm waters. He is humming "Redemption Song," a Bob Marley tune, as he pantomimes the motions of baptizing and scrubbing himself clean.

Carlton decides that he is going in too. He quickly strips down, hesitates for a second, and then he peels off his jockey shorts. He lets out a long loud yell, dives naked into the warm waters and swims past his father, out into the deep swells.

"You talk to him, Mr. Richard," Maxine giggles into the phone. "The boy insists that I'm trying to poison your mammy. This oil does work miracles. See if you can get him to see the sense."

Richard has the actor's trick of changing his voice to suit. With Maxine he is the handsome young man she remembers from when she first started working for his mother. With me, he has opted for his award-winning infomercial voice, with a little dose of Trinidad patois.

"What can be the harm?" Richard sides with Maxine. "If she believe in the stuff half as much as Maxine, it bound to do her some good, man."

"Faith does move more mountains than medicines." Maxine is working from the same script as Richard. "I went to a lot of trouble to get the oil for your Auntie." Maxine shakes her head with wonder at how I could be so ungrateful?

Auntie Vere's health has taken a turn for the worse, and Maxine believes that the black market oil from old electrical transformers has special properties. This is based on the scientific method — "that all the irons and salts in transformer oil have been well and truly charged up."

Electrical transformers are also filled with PCBs that are highly toxic, and are known to cause cancer. I explain all of this loudly to Richard, and for Maxine's benefit. As the only flesh and blood member of Auntie Vere's family present, I feel I have to stand firm and express what I think is the best for her. But I know that Maxine will do whatever she thinks best in the end.

"I have a top specialist all lined up," Richard says.

"I don't think she will ever be well enough to fly," I say. But Richard doesn't want to hear the truth about his mother's failing health.

"Tell Mr. Richard his mammy time near," Maxine adds her plea.

It is impossible, Richard insists, for him to get away. Richard has never been back to Trinidad. This is attributed to his sensitive nature, hinted at in the gossip of my mother and her cousins, to the horrors he must have had to face, growing up gay in Trinidad.

"Some people when they leave, they leave for good." Maxine has the last word on this. "And they never come back, not for money, not for love."

Auntie Vere is weak, but fully composed. She has sent for her solicitor. She has business to fix up, and a bone to pick with that ungrateful scamp.

Mr. Boone, the solicitor, has been intercepted by Roberts. I get the sense that they know each other. Roberts is attempting to pick Mr. Boone's brains on Carlton's behalf.

"I'm the wrong man to ask." Mr. Boone is cautiously polite with Roberts. "That is not my area of expertise at all. Is a complicated case, man. The best advice is to get the right advice.

"How the old girl doing?" Mr. Boone, the solicitor, becomes Boots the old family friend. "I'm glad she catch me before I gone," Boots says. He is "pulling up stumps" to return to England, and no one is more surprised at this than Boots. It surprises me too. I had Boots pegged as a relic from colonial England — a type that used to wash up regularly on the shores of the island: the expatriate sort, who prefers a comfortable exile to an anonymous return.

"When I first came out, I thought six months to a year. Don't ask me where the time went," he says. But something is pulling him back. Nostalgia? No, not that, Boots has considered every argument. He has had "a good inning," he has "made his mark in Trinidad," and now he "simply wants to go home."

"You must know what I mean?" he says.

Boots is under the impression that I am back for good. I can see how that can happen, especially with Auntie Vere as the source.

"No place sweeter than home," Boots says. He looks at me and I agree. I give him the reassurance he wants.

My mother and her cousins are the reasons why long distance phone companies are in business, and making obscene profits. I'm sure one or more of them could have flown down to Trinidad already, and sized up the situation for themselves. The latest talk is that Richard's wife, Denise, is planning to fly down, but this is dismissed as a ploy to get Richard involved.

"I not asking anybody to fly down, and I not stopping anybody," is Auntie Vere's official position. "Soon is my time to meet the Lord. And I not getting on no airplane for that." Auntie Vere insists that I "relay that message for me please."

A contingent of cousins is slated to arrive and I am given a new assignment; I'm to help Maxine with "the preparations." This seems to consist of my double-checking on and getting in Maxine's way. Auntie Vere is now frequently unstuck in time, and I get to

play the roles of her Russell, her Richard, and her famous conductor lover. Whenever we get to the part of the loop where I can
play myself, we go over the same recent ground, and I find it somehow easier to have the same conversation over and over again.

"How was your trip to Point?" Auntie Vere asks.

"Good, good," I say. "I went to Cedros."

"Did you find what you were looking for, boy?" Auntie Vere
asks.

"No, I didn't see any pirates this time, Auntie." I play along.

"Boy," Auntie Vere says. "What I tell you? You must keep your
eyes peeled. This place is still full of old pirates, yes."

If it is, I can't find them anymore.

"You see how some things does change all of a sudden and in a
hurry, boy?" Auntie Vere goes in through one door and comes out
from another. "But some things does remain in place. And is only
you, who really move."

Roberts and Carlton have gone into business together; they oper-
ate a taxi service. Roberts and son have done a tidy business ferry-
ing the cousins in from the airport for Auntie Vere's funeral. Carlton has modified his father's chauffeur's uniform. He has retained
the Greek fisherman's cap, but his sits higher up on his stringy
dreadlocks. And he has discarded the pocket crest in favour of a
narrow black tie with a long-sleeved white shirt. Roberts tells me
with parental pride how Carlton approaches businessmen at the
airport, "and with his Canadian accent, he can sweet talk too bad."

"Once you have an in," Carlton says, patting his pocket pager,
"you can get work for days." Not only is Carlton looking more and
more like his father, he's sounding like him too.

My audit is quite complete: there is no buried treasure. The
company I work for has decided to scuttle this ship immediately.
This lets me out of making the decision to stay on in Trinidad.
And now it's my turn to go, but I have one last assignment to complete.

The cousins are massed like a choir in Auntie Vere's music

practice room. They insist on a group photograph to commemorate the occasion. My mother is of course front and centre, the conductor. "Make sure everybody squeeze in good and tight, tell us when to say 'cheese please, Louise.'"

The cousins shuffle and switch places around the piano. In this version of musical chairs no one wants to sit in Auntie Vere's spot on the piano bench.

"Wait, wait." My mother does a head count; somebody is missing. "Maxine, come come."

Maxine comes from her kitchen, but only to the doorway. She is still wearing her good clothes from the funeral, but with an apron.

"I have something in the oven to watch out for." Maxine shyly backs away. The chorus swells in unison until Maxine agrees to join them, at the edge of the semi-circle. I ask her to move in closer.

"If it's all the same, I would prefer to sit down, please." Maxine moves the piano bench back carefully and seats herself squarely. She folds her hands in her lap and straightens her back; she studies the black and white keys intently and now she extends her arms full stretch with her fingers locked. Slowly she raises her hands above her head, straightens her elbows, and holds the pose that completes this ritual that she must have observed a thousand times.

"If Miss Vere was to see me now," Maxine says, "is mad she must think that I surely gone mad." The chorus of cousins breaks out laughing. That is the instant that I snap the photograph. At the last moment, I've found some treasure to take with me, after all.

There Used To Be
a River Here

I'm the safety officer at the Pearl River mine. I've got my Industrial First Aid and my HAZMAT ticket. How that qualifies me to handle a situation like this I surely don't know, but I'm in charge until the weather breaks and someone from the coroner's office and the police can get up here.

As safety officer, I keep track of all the accidents at the mine. I've had to deal with fatalities before, but never something like this. I've had to tell wives with young children, and families — one as far away as Italy — that someone they love is gone. They all want to know how it happened. I have a file full of letters from lawyers and insurance companies, and I have learned how to choose phrases from all that careful language and make them my own. I have always sent deep regret and hope for a better future.

What do I say now, about a situation like this? The police sergeant I spoke to on the phone said not to jump to any conclusions, and not to touch anything. Just describe what you see; write everything down. What I see is a great big mess. We've got a dead girl, and a dead boy, both with half their heads blown off.

The girl's name is Denise Eckles, which I didn't know. Everyone called her Kit. And she worked for the Chinaman, Milton T'sang. She was twenty. Which seems like hardly any time at all, for a life.

Milton's last name is spelled with a T apostrophe, which I also didn't know, until I started making out this report. Milton found them. Kit didn't show up for work, and it took three days for Milton's patience to run out. He went to see what was what, and now he wishes he hadn't been the one to find them. A thing like this you don't want to see for yourself. I surely would have preferred not to see it; I could live without the knowledge of such a thing.

The boy's name is Jesse Hallsey. Jesse was called Jaycee by everyone, and he was twenty-two. He was the son of Albert Hallsey, who is the general foreman of the mine. Which makes him my boss. No one could expect a man to take charge of a thing like this, that involves his own son.

I don't know how far back I should go for my report, so I'll just start with around the time when Kit got here. I suppose it's a fair enough place to begin.

Last May, Jaycee came home from school. He brought along a crew of four young guys like himself, and Kit. They drove straight through, taking turns in two vehicles, one of which was a VW van. The VW was more of a conversion than a camper, and I can't say for sure who owned it, but Kit lived in it all summer.

The boys all got jobs at the mine, and Kit went to work for Milton. It doesn't sound right to say it, me not wanting to speak ill of the dead and all, but I heard those boys all had their turn with Kit. I'm not passing judgement here, but that's the kind of thing I suppose I should make mention of. I can't think of a delicate way to put this, but Kit fucked like a man. By that I mean she would fuck without conscience or worry as to the consequence about whom she might offend, or who might think the less of her for it. It didn't make Kit all too popular with the other women up here. Women are a scarce commodity in Pearl River, and the ones who live up here are all married or accounted for in some way.

A free agent like Kit caused a lot of clucking, but that didn't seem to bother her in the least. I'm not going to go on like some old-timer, about "the kids today — they've got no shame or decency." They're like birds that land on the same branch, they flit and flap and go at it like robins, but none of it is too serious. I wish I could say that it was jealousy or trouble over sex, but there were no signs of that. I don't know what the cause of this thing was.

At the end of summer the boys all went back to school, except for Jaycee, and Kit stayed on to work for Milton. Jaycee said he was finished with school, which didn't make Albert — his dad — none too pleased. Jaycee had only one semester left to graduate, and he didn't offer any reason why or talk about some other plan. That sort of thing would be troubling to any parent, but especially so to a straight arrow like Albert Hallsey.

Albert Hallsey is a miner. There are two basic kinds of miners. One kind goes out prospecting and trips over the stuff — usually in the worst sort of bush. The other kind, the stubborn ones, have to figure out a way to wrestle it from underground, and get it out of the bush. When Albert Hallsey came up to run the Pearl River mine, it had already gone under twice, and changed hands three times. Albert's been in charge for fourteen years now; the mine has changed hands a couple more times, and so far as I know, it has only ever made money twice. This is how it is in mining: you hold the thing together with baling wire and a line of credit, and hope that when a spike in price comes, you're ready.

It's fair comment to say that Pearl River cost Albert Hallsey his marriage; I don't know what to say about what happened to his son. I don't have the expertise to say how or why a thing like this happens, and that's all that I'm putting in my report. When the police and the coroner get here, they can go about their business, let them sort it out, and let them decide — what? Dead is dead.

The weather finally broke, long enough for a plane to land with

the coroner, a uniform policeman and a plainclothes policeman.
I took a dislike to the plainclothes right away. Some people just
rub me the wrong way right off, and I won't apologize for that. No
sir! And I can't think of too many times when I've had to back up
and reverse my thinking.

The coroner looks like a Christmas tree ornament in her bright
red parka and white moon boots; she's some kind of Oriental woman, no more than five feet tall. Milton got all excited when she
came into his restaurant; he talked to her in some Chinese lingo,
and she answered him back in Chinese, but then they switched
over to English.

Milton went and got out his fancy teapot and his good tea for
her. And he put on some of that squeaky opera-sounding music
he likes to listen to when no one else is in the restaurant. The
plainclothes told Milton to "turn that shit off." Boom — just like
that. No if you please and thanks. You could see on Milton's face
how his pressure took a spike. But Milton didn't make his money
by arguing, and if I was this clown, I'd be extra careful about what
I ate in Milton's restaurant.

The uniform policeman is regulation issue: a big sandy-haired
guy who should think again about sporting that walrus mustache.
He's the kind of policeman who keeps the peace by bringing the
idea of extreme force to the table.

"A hot coffee would go down good, right about now," the uniform policeman says. He stands up and gets the plainclothes to
stand up along with him. "What do we do around here? Fix our
own?"

Milton just nods and does that thing that Chinamen do: he
draws into some sort of space around himself. The coroner lifts
her teacup, has a sip, and gives Milton a nod, so slight, it's hard to
say if or what she is commenting on. The pilot comes in with
some parcels. Milton is also the postmaster, and he goes about his
business.

In Pearl River, any fresh female face comes in for close scrutiny.
The coroner has curious hair, exactly equal parts black and silver,

depending on how she turns to the light. With that smooth almost unlined face, I couldn't even begin to guess which side of forty. There's still something girlish about her, and I wonder if she is married or single. How do you go home to a loved one — "Hi honey, how was your day?" — after seeing the things she must see in a job like hers? You're bound to get all crossed up over human nature.

"How'd you get into this line of work?" I ask.

"I have a background in medicine," the coroner replies.

"Been doing it long?"

"Long enough to know I won't do it forever."

"I have a report," I say. "Nothing fancy, just who, and where, and when they were found. I don't really know what else I should put down."

"I'm sure your report is just fine."

"I'm not sure what all else is expected," I add.

"When something like this happens in a remote community, we don't want you people to start thinking that you're outside the law. Or that you're not entitled to the full process of the law. We put on a show."

I can't decide which side of funny to place her. But I've been dealing with the situation for a couple of days now, and I'm real eager to put the whole thing in somebody else's hands.

"What comes next?" I ask.

"The police have their thing to do. And I have mine. The first phase is what we call discovery. We examine the bodies, where and how they were found. And then we decide whether to call a hearing for information. After that we go away and write up a report. In an instance like this, we'll most likely have to wait for the autopsy results. Sometimes there's a formal hearing at the end, an inquest, if it's in the public interest."

"How far out of town is it?" The uniform policeman approaches us.

"Let's get to the scene." The plainclothes is raring to go.

I make the case for leaving it until morning. "The weather's come up again. It's at least half an hour, and it'll be dark, time we get out there. You don't want to do this in the dark?"

I don't know what the pecking order between the coroner and the police is, but as far as I'm concerned, the coroner is the one in charge. Finally we all turn to her. The coroner continues to sip her tea.

"Will they still be dead in the morning?" she asks dryly.

Milton didn't set out to name the town Pearl River. All he was after was a name for his motel and restaurant business, which he set up in the five trailers he bought for a hundred dollars total, from the company that built the mine. The hundred dollars was just a formality to get the trailers legally off the books. It was a hundred-dollar joke, at the expense of some crazy Chinaman who thought he could open a motel five miles from nowhere. That was eighteen years ago. Pearl River is a town of about six hundred now, and that can swell to near a thousand in the summer when the mine is running flat out. There's some fishing and some hunting traffic, well into the fall until freeze-up. Milton does better than all right.

Back in the fall, Kit moved out of the VW camper and into an abandoned cabin. The cabin was never much; it was built years ago on Crown lease land. I've heard tall tales about fishing from bed: how you could cast from the window and reel a fish straight into your frying pan. There used to be a river here, but when the mine expanded, the river was diverted, and more than a few cabins were left high and dry.

Kit wasn't the best waitress I ever saw for looks or for how she handled the work, but she was easy enough on the eyes, and she didn't slack on the job. Kit was never short of company when she wanted it. I heard stories about the parties she had out there at the cabin, but it never bothered me that some people were having more of a time. I've had my day. At the end of the summer, after the boys left, Kit was still a hot topic of conversation. It took a certain amount of craziness I suppose, to live alone in a cabin way out there, especially after freeze-up.

Albert's boy, Jaycee, belonged to all of us. This sort of life is not for everyone. There are other children here in Pearl River now, but back when Albert Hallsey first came up to run things, his son was a rare and curious boy. One time when Jaycee was no more than ten, he wandered off, and the whole town went out looking for him.

When Albert found him, he was fishing the river. Albert asked Jaycee if he hadn't heard us hollering? And why didn't he answer? Jaycee replied, "The fish are biting." He didn't want us scaring them away.

I've known Albert Hallsey longer than most, but I can't say better than most. Albert is the sort of man who takes the responsibility of being the general foreman everywhere with him. The big thing with Albert is to be scrupulously fair, and somehow that doesn't allow the man to have any latitude. Not even with his own son. Albert was always strict with Jaycee, and Jaycee never bucked against that in the way most kids eventually do. Last fall, when Jaycee flat out refused to go back and finish up at school, that was a first. And maybe, in hindsight, it was some kind of sign?

It's not fair to say that Albert was trying to punish Jaycee by laying him off, right before Christmas. Albert does everything he can to keep the mine running, and share the work around. And so what if he wanted to teach his son a hard lesson? Get him to go back and finish up school — who can blame him for that?

Jaycee had been sitting around idle for some weeks. I'd see him at Milton's stretching out a coffee until Kit got off work. I can't recall the exact dates or instances, but I'd seen the two of them tearing around in his pickup. When a thing like this happens, you look back to see if there were signs that were missed. I can't say that I saw anything coming. At this time of year, there's the usual talk about cabin fever, but no one in Pearl River can claim that they foresaw this.

The weather has let up some — it's the kind of day where if it weren't so damn cold, you'd swear you were in some sort of winter paradise. Not that anybody is paying all that much attention to the snow and the scenery now that we've reached the cabin.

A blanket of new snow covers everything. It's drifted and piled up deep against the cabin. We have some work to do to get the door open. As soon as we're inside the uniform policeman pulls out a camera of a type I've never seen before. He sees me wondering, and he tells me that it's digital. I know that means something to do with computers. He's taking pictures from all angles, and I'm thinking that's a hell of a job. How that must burn the whole scene into your brain in a hard-to-forget sort of way.

The plainclothes uses a little tape recorder, no bigger than his hand. He makes a comment, and then he shuts it off. He'd say something like, "Distance from cabin door to first body, measuring now." Off. On. "Distance nine feet." Off. He has a clear series of things he's supposed to do, and I can tell there's some sort of order to his approach.

I can't figure out what the coroner is supposed to be doing. It looks like she's meditating, and then I realize that she must have to wait for the other two to get their licks in first.

There's not a whole lot of room in the cabin to begin with. Anytime any one of the four of us makes a move, it causes confusion. I'm real curious to see how they do what they do, to see what they can figure out, but the plainclothes tells me flat out to go and wait in my truck.

The best part of an hour goes by, and just when I decide to get out and have a pee and a stretch, the policeman and the plainclothes come outside to the truck.

"Did you look around for a note?" the plainclothes asks.

I did think to look for a note. But I'm not saying anything if I can help it to make his job easier. The scene inside has sobered him up. I wouldn't say he is courteous, but he's closer to polite.

"What do we do? Take the bodies back in your truck?" He's only asking out of formality; the uniform policeman is already unpacking the gear they'll need. The cold weather must help in a case like this. But still, there's a lot of scraping up and sorting out, and I'm relieved that I don't have to do it.

The coroner is the only one still inside the cabin; it's her turn to do her thing, I guess. And we're waiting for her to give the all-clear signal. It's only a few minutes, but those are some long minutes. The two policemen go in and bring the body bags out. And then another bag with the bits. They do a last minute sorting out, double-check of tools and equipment, and we are all set to go, except for the coroner, who is still inside the cabin.

"Why the hell did she say she was ready?" The plainclothes is working up a head of useless steam. I have an understanding now, how a job like his can set you on edge, but I still think he doesn't have to be such a jackass.

When the coroner finally comes out, she takes a stick and pokes some holes in the snow. Then she heads in the direction of the outhouse and she's bent over nearly double. I'm thinking either Milton's cooking or something else has gotten to her, but she's not in any such distress. Next she walks around close beside the cabin and tries to jump up and look in the window. She slips and falls and gives a little scream of surprise. Now she digs her mitts into the snow and makes a snowball, which she rears back and wings with all her might. It wobbles like a lame duck and dies before it hits the cabin.

"What the hell is she doing now?" the plainclothes fumes.

"She does go about it a little different," the uniform policeman allows. "But in all fairness, she knows her stuff."

The coroner dusts the snow off her parka and works her way back to the truck.

"I have everything I need. Are you ready?" the coroner asks.

The other two nod. We get in the truck. And head back to town.

There's quite a crowd inside Milton's restaurant: more than half the town has suddenly decided that it's urgent to check their mail.

Albert Hallsey is here. And so is his secretary, Hélène Mills. I'm surprised to see Hélène, and until now Albert has stayed out of it. But I suppose he wants to know what the coroner and the police have to say about what happened in the cabin.

The coroner and the two policemen go over their notes. Then they have a quick conference. I can't hear exactly what, but it's no surprise that the plainclothes doesn't like it. The coroner says something to Milton in Chinese, and Milton nods and sidles away. The next thing you know he's rearranging his restaurant into a temporary hearing room. The uniform policeman seems to know this drill, and he helps Milton with the seating arrangements. People have been filing in for some time. By the time the coroner signals for Milton to bar the door, it's standing room only. The uniform policeman acts like a bailiff; he shushes everyone and calls the hearing to order.

"I am the advocate for the dead." The coroner knows this speech by heart. "As such, I am charged with examining the circumstances and the reasons for any and all deaths, and especially so, for any deaths of an unusual or unnatural occurrence. This is a hearing for information, not cause."

The coroner sits down. The plainclothes policeman takes over.

"We will begin by establishing the sequence of events, surrounding the discovery of the bodies. Milton T. Sang? Will you step forward?"

Milton shuffles forward to take his seat. The coroner says something in Chinese, and Milton's face reddens.

"Please note the correct spelling of Mr. T'sang's surname. The T is silent." The coroner is making it clear to all that she's in charge. The uniform policeman, who is recording the proceedings, looks puzzled and then he catches on. He scribbles the correction in his notebook.

"Mr. T'sang?" the plainclothes asks, "you discovered the bodies?"

Milton nods.

"You went out to the cabin? Why?"

"Just like I told to him," Milton points to me. "I wait for Kit.

Three whole days. Kit no show. No work. I go see. I find. Big mess. They dead. I come back to town. I call mine office."

"Who did you speak to?"

"I speak to secretary. I ask for boss. I tell her bad thing happen with boy and Kit."

"Then what did you do?" the plainclothes asks.

Milton sits reflecting on this question for quite some time.

"Mr. T'sang?" the coroner prompts. Milton turns to face away from the coroner and the plainclothes; he looks out and past the hushed crowd in his restaurant.

"I cry. I cry. For Kit. So young. I cry so long. For Kit."

Milton is excused.

Hélène Mills' turn is next. Hélène is the secretary for the mine. She's a Catholic, and she wants to know if she can "swear in on a Christian bible?" Hélène is nervous and proper by nature, and she wasn't expecting this moment in the full spotlight. She keeps looking towards Albert for some reassurance. Hélène is in one of those marriages that's all over except for the divorce papers. It's nobody's business, but Hélène and Albert have a relationship that extends beyond the mine's office.

"It's pretty much what Milton said. I went and saw Albert — Mr. Hallsey. Good thing he was already sitting down. I couldn't bear to tell him. But he took one look at me and he knew something serious was wrong." Hélène looks over at Albert who nods his confirmation. Hélène takes a deep breath, and expels her next line. "I told Mr. Hallsey there'd been some sort of accident and Jaycee was dead."

Hélène bows her head. Even now she still can't stand to be the bearer of such news. Hélène is relieved to step down.

Albert Hallsey steps forward. This is the first I've seen of Albert since the cabin. You don't have to see blood or bandages to know when a man is wounded. He looks like someone who's lost something he has no hope of ever finding.

"I drove straight away out to the cabin," Albert says. "I told the safety officer to meet me there."

"You called the safety officer?" The plainclothes policeman steps into the line of questioning. "Before you drove straight out?"

"Yes," Albert confirms. "I told him to meet me there."

Hélène came and told me. She told me that Albert said for me to meet him at the cabin. It's a small discrepancy. And I'm wondering if I should bother to correct it when it's my turn.

"The safety officer was at the mine?" The plainclothes is sniffing at something, "Why didn't you just wait and go together?"

Albert looks at the plainclothes; he must hear the insinuation also. There's a change in his tone. "I went to my son as quickly as I could."

"Was the safety officer there?" the plainclothes asks, "when you arrived?"

"No, I got there first."

"And then, what did you do?" The plainclothes insists on taking it step by step.

"I looked inside."

"Did you look inside? Or go inside?" the plainclothes asks.

"I went inside and looked."

"What exactly did you see?"

"I saw the bodies. The two bodies."

"What did you do then?" the plainclothes asks. "What did you do next?"

"I don't remember much," Albert says, "after that."

The plainclothes fishes around under his table, he unzips a large case and takes out a clear plastic bag. It's as plain as day what's inside the bag.

The plainclothes walks back over to Albert.

"Is this your son's rifle?" The plainclothes turns the rifle slowly in the bag.

"It's mine," Albert says in a hoarse whisper. He barely looks at the rifle.

"Did you touch anything? Did you move anything about, inside the cabin?" The plainclothes walks over to his table and puts the rifle back in its case.

"I don't remember what I did," Albert says. "I guess I was in shock. I went and sat in my truck."

"Do you remember anything else?" the plainclothes asks again. There is no need for him to ride Albert hard like this. The man has lost his son.

"You waited in your truck for the safety officer?" the coroner interjects. She has decided that enough is enough. The plainclothes doesn't look too pleased about that.

Albert looks at the coroner with some small relief, and then at me to confirm this. I nod. He wasn't in his truck when I got there. He was waist deep in the snow, in the old bed where the river used to be.

Albert steps down. I'm next.

"What did you do?" the plainclothes asks. "What did you see?"

I confirmed Albert's story. It didn't take long for me to add my piece; basically I just read what was in my report. The coroner then asked the uniform policeman and the plainclothes if they had anything else to add. The uniform said that he was satisfied with the proceedings. The plainclothes said that he would reserve his comment until he received the ballistics report, and a copy of the autopsies.

"Does anyone want to make a statement of impact?" The coroner has one last formality to complete before she brings the hearing for information to a close. The crowd inside Milton's goes real quiet, as if everyone's considering. What sort of impact does a thing like this create? How do you even begin to measure the loss of what used to be? And how do you measure that against what could have been?

The pilot and Milton are bickering over some items of freight. The pilot says he can't take it all on this run. How he's already carrying too much dead weight as it is, and how he's not taking any chances in this sort of weather. Milton is not satisfied with this answer. He says he knows that the pilot is packing lots of moose meat for some hunters. The post office parcels come first, Milton insists. He has a guarantee. The pilot tells Milton the hunters have a better guarantee — cash money. Milton is not going to beat that, and he gives up the argument and retreats to his kitchen.

The uniform policeman is curious about the local fishing, and says how he might make it back up here, one day. The plainclothes is off the clock, but still tightly wound; he makes no secret of his impatience.

"Dead people don't wipe their fingerprints off a rifle. We can make a fair guess now, but once we get the ballistics we'll know exactly what happened. And we'll know who tampered with what. There'll be charges laid all right, interfering with a body, and withholding evidence." The plainclothes is doing his best to rattle me.

"You don't say?" I dare him right back.

"Don't say anything else," the uniform policeman says to the plainclothes. "This is an active case. You know better."

"I know what my job is," the plainclothes snaps at the uniform policeman. I can't see him lasting too much longer in this line of work. "She's the one who's covering up."

"I am not covering anything up," the coroner says lowering her voice. "Are you trying to tell me how to do my job? I have a report to write. And so do you."

"If I contradict you, it goes nowhere. You're the coroner. You always have the final word," the plainclothes says with some bitterness.

"That's not so," the coroner keeps her voice level, "not if it is a criminal matter."

"How do you know it isn't?" The plainclothes scowls at her.

"I *know* what happened." The coroner stares the plainclothes down.

"And I don't?" the plainclothes sneers at her.

"Don't tell me how to do my job." The coroner's voice rises. "I am the advocate for the dead. You still don't understand what that means, do you? I work for the dead. I am required, in fact, I am compelled by the law, to act in the best interests of the dead."

"How can you say that if you leave this unchallenged?" the plainclothes says.

"You're so way off, you don't even know it," the coroner says.

"You're questioning how I do my job?" The plainclothes is more than ready to get into it. "Why don't we settle this? Right here. Right now. Send for Albert Hallsey. I'll nail him down in five minutes."

The coroner sips her tea, and then she takes the lid off the teapot and places it upside down on the table. Which must give Milton some sort of signal, because he comes over in a minute to refill her teapot.

"Would you please sit down, for a moment, Mr. T'sang?" the coroner requests.

Milton begs to be excused. The coroner insists. The uniform policeman stands up. The coroner looks at Milton. Milton looks like he's been half expecting this, and he sits down.

"What exactly did you do at the cabin?" The coroner chooses her words and her tone carefully. Milton starts to rattle something off in Chinese, but the coroner calls a halt to that right away.

"Tell the truth; tell me everything," the coroner says sharply.

Milton hesitates, and then he starts back up in English.

"First I see naked boy. Then Kit. Kit naked too. I go outside. Quick. I try to think. What to do? What?

"I see Kit in my mind. Kit so full of laughs. Kit so sad sometimes. Kit go with lots of boys, I know. I know that. Kit is a good girl. Kit still a good girl.

"Kit look so ugly like that. So naked. I put clothes on, for Kit. I put Kit in bed. I try to fix Kit up, a little bit, but her head — very bad damage."

"You put her in the bed?" the plainclothes asks, astounded.

"Yes," Milton says. "I try to move boy, to chair, but he too heavy."

"What the hell did you do that for?" the plainclothes asks. He is pissed off. "Were you planning a flipping tea party?"

Milton looks at the coroner, he's trembling, but in such a way that I think he's grateful for the release.

"Then I come back to town. Then I call mine."

"Well, that accounts for some of the discrepancies, but there's more physical evidence of disturbance. It still doesn't add up." The plainclothes is still not satisfied.

"Are you ready to tell what happened?" The coroner asks, turning to me. "Or do I have to bring your boss, Albert Hallsey, back in?"

"Leave Albert be," I say. "I'll tell the rest." I had gone over it often enough in my own mind, so it was easy to tell.

Hélène had come to get a hold of me. She was blubbering, and a mess. She told me something terrible had happened. Jaycee was dead. Him and that new waitress from Milton's. Albert's already gone out to the cabin, she said. He wants you to meet him out there. I knew what she was saying must be true, but I didn't want to believe it just yet. I put the truth of it aside until I got there. I had to see it for myself. I told myself to drive careful, don't go adding more trouble on top of trouble.

When I arrived, Albert's truck was parked at a sharp angle to Jaycee's truck. I pulled mine in tight, in line with Albert's. I could feel the snow crunch under my boots as if I were stepping on crushed glass. The door to the cabin was wide open, and I could see a body propped up in an unnatural fashion against a chair. I stood in the doorway, not wanting to enter until I was sure that whatever had done and caused a thing like this, was gone.

Albert was not inside. I entered. And I crossed over to the bed. I had to make sure. It was Kit on the bed. She was laid out, all nice and natural, and I wanted to think otherwise, that she was just asleep, but I never believed it for a second. Then I saw what was left of her face: she was surely dead. The truth of it hit me right then and there.

I went outside to look for Albert. I followed his tracks. His footsteps ended in a reel of confusion near his truck, and then I saw where he slipped and slid down the embankment. He had ploughed on, out to the old riverbed, and he was waist deep in the snow.

"What are you doing?" I called out to Albert.

"Jaycee is lost," Albert said.

"He's in the cabin, Albert," I said.

"No," Albert said. "No, he's lost."

It took some doing to get Albert turned around, and back to his truck. We had the heater running for some minutes but nothing was going to take away that kind of chill.

"What's it look like to you?" Albert finally asked.

I said it didn't look good at all.

"It looks like Jaycee did it," Albert said. "Looks like he killed that girl, and himself."

I had to admit that it looked like that to me too.

"I don't see why he had to do a thing like that?" Albert said. "I don't see why he had to kill the girl, too? I don't know how to live with that."

I couldn't accept it either. And surely no one could expect a man to take charge of a thing like this, that involved his own son. I told Albert to wait in his truck. I didn't want him driving back by himself. I went back inside the cabin. And I tried to tidy things up. I moved the bodies around. I tried to make it look like a double suicide. I did it all wrong, I suppose, but I only did it to fix something that surely was not right.

When I had finished, the plainclothes is even more ticked-off. "What the hell is the matter with you people up here?" he shouts. He wants to charge me with obstruction and tampering with the evidence.

"You and Albert Hallsey were wrong," the coroner says, turning to me. "Any time a weapon is fired it leaves a trace. We know they *both* fired the rifle. What we don't know yet is who fired first. This kind of cold slows things down. It's going to be difficult to say how much time elapsed between the first and second shots. They may have made a pact and done it together. Or the boy could have come in on the scene hours later. If I had to guess right now, I'd say the girl went first. It was a double suicide all along." She was sure the ballistics would confirm it. "The dead would be best served, if it were written up as such."

The uniform policeman says that he can see "no criminal intent on my part, or Milton's for that matter," and he would write it up like that. It is two against one, and the plainclothes doesn't come right out and say so, but I feel like he is going to go along.

"What happened to those kids?" The plainclothes policeman finally says it out loud. He asks the one question that hangs over all of this. The strain of his job shows all over his face. "Why blow your brains out like that?" The plainclothes can't leave it be.

It goes real quiet in Milton's restaurant; everyone is chewing on the same thing.

"Maybe it's the isolation?" The uniform policeman takes a step towards the coffee pot. "The suicide rate is consistently higher, right across the north."

The plainclothes also gets up. He moves around the room. He's practically doing jumping jacks; he waves his arms about as if he's trying to disperse a cloud.

"Don't you have some leave coming to you?" The coroner pushes her teacup away.

The pilot comes back to say he's ready, and we all go outside. Milton and the pilot have come to some arrangement over the parcels, and the last items are stowed. A small crowd gathers — the kind of people who have plenty to say but nothing to add. Some are nosey enough to take a look in the back, so they can say later on that they saw the bodies.

"Don't go around thinking that you're outside the law, up here," the coroner warns me.

I nod, but I think to myself that there's punishment enough for the living to go on living, without assigning more blame.

Albert Hallsey goes walking past Milton's restaurant with Hélène. She holds on to his arm, forgetting for once all those who might see them out together in public. She and Albert walk by without slowing or stopping. Albert never looks inside.

Fifteen Fingers

I do a little skip tracing when things are slow. This job is not too far off that line. It's a locate and verify for a law firm. I ring the doorbell and take a step back.

"Yes? I'm Dorothy Gail Lynch. Crystal Gail is my stage name . . . Gail Miller? That was two husbands ago. I never got around to changing it . . . Do I know a Robert Northrop Haywood? The last I saw of Robert was ages and ages ago . . . Really. I was still doing Holiday Inns. Whatever has become of Robert Haywood?"

I've never hit upon a good way to break it to people. I suppose it's best to just get it said, and then give a moment of silence.

". . . Sorry for your loss," I say.

"Oh, no," she says, and then looks at her watch. "It's too late for sherry. Thank God." She motions for me to come in and join her in a drink. "Scotch?"

Crystal Gail is the theatrical sort. It's hard to know if she's chatting me up or playing to me. Either way, I have no objections. She's a vintage bit of English bird, and she's done her best to keep her feathers trim.

"I ruin mine with ice," she says. "How do you like it?" I get the feeling she's measuring more than the drink.

"Ice is nice," is all I can think of to say.

"Oh really," Crystal Gail says with a throaty kind of laugh, and I decide to play out the little that I know for as long as I can, and see how far it gets me. "How did you meet Robert Haywood?"

"We're both of us from Brighton. Robert was the brightest boy in all of Brighton. That's what it said in the papers after he won some great big scholarship. That was why the Pounds hired him as a tutor for their kiddies. Always get the best, and never you mind the cost, it'll pay off in the end. That was the Pounds' style.

"The Pounds owned the Hearthstone Hotel in Brighton. Billy Morris and his band, the Blues Angels, headlined the pub. Billy Morris made me take voice and piano lessons from his sister, and took it out of my pay! Still, Billy gave me my start, and I suppose I should be eternally grateful for that.

"I did two sets with Billy Morris in the pub. I only had to sing for my supper, but poor Robert — he had the more difficult job — he had to tutor the little shillings and pence for their O Levels. We took our staff meals together, and Robert would stick around to hear me sing, and for the chance to walk me home. Robert followed me to Canada, Robert did. He was sweet on me, Robert, he was. I never thought I gave him that much encouragement, not really — "

"It seems he's left you something in his will, Mrs. Miller."

If I don't stop her she'll go on all night.

"Robert was always such a dear." I have her full and suspicious attention now. "What exactly did he leave me?"

"Mrs. Miller, soon you'll get a letter from a law firm, asking you for proof. They'll want to know that you are in fact Dorothy Gail Lynch, and they'll want you to establish your connection to Robert Northrop Haywood."

"Why?" Crystal Gail has had her share of hard knocks. "This can't cause me any trouble, can it?"

"Here's the card for the lawyers," I say. "You can call them yourself, but you'd probably do well to talk to a different set of lawyers, before you sign off on anything. I've already said more than I should've, Mrs. Miller."

Robert Northrop Haywood excelled in mathematics. He won scholarships, which was fortunate and necessary. On one of those desperate times, when his dad went up to London to look for a better way, his mum died. And Robert was essentially on his own from fourteen on. It was hardscrabble, until the Pounds, a family with aspirations, hired him as a tutor, hoping that some of his brilliance would somehow rub off on their little "shillings and pence." It was a job that suited him; it included a staff meal at the Pounds' hotel, and later on, a pint of beer in the hotel's pub.

Robert Northrop Haywood was not the first man to fall for a singer in a pub. And he won't be the last man to go searching after a girl with only love as his beacon. His quest brought him to Canada, where his Dorothy had hardened into Crystal Gail. And in the lobby of a Holiday Inn, in all that anonymous coming and going, his heart was well and truly broken.

At that time, anyone with a couple of letters after their name from an English university could land themselves a teaching job. When Robert Northrop Haywood, a promising young mathematician, was offered a position teaching economics, he decided to stay on in Canada.

"What do I get?" Crystal Gail got right to the point.

Crystal asked me to accompany her to the lawyer's office. I can tell that the lawyer is not thrilled with my being there. And I can pretty much kiss off any chance of doing any more work for his firm.

"We do not know what you will get, Mrs. Miller," the lawyer says in that special tone that they reserve for people who irritate them. "There is some question about what you may or may not hold."

"Didn't you ask me to come in right away?" Crystal Gail has stared down hecklers and fended off drunks. A hiss-polite lawyer is not going to throw her.

"The executors of Dr. Haywood's estate wish to assemble a selection of his unpublished papers. It seems that Dr. Haywood shared the credit to some of his early work with you. The university where he worked has contested your ownership of the copyright. It is their contention that these papers were a part of his research, and, as he was employed and compensated by the university for this research . . . the findings of said research, are also the property of the university."

"I don't get it?" Crystal says. "Robert has left me some old papers? There's no money?"

"Well, no and yes." The lawyer gives the kind of answer that only lawyers can give with a straight face. "Mrs. Miller, the executors are prepared to offer you a very significant token to release any claim to copyright of these papers."

"What?" my curiosity gets the better of me, "is a very significant token?"

"Mrs. Miller," the lawyer replies, totally ignoring me, "the university is in a bit of a bind. Their intention is to compile Dr. Haywood's early work as a posthumous tribute. But this was before any knowledge of copyright concerns emerged."

I hope Crystal sees that she's got leverage.

"So, it's like you've cut an album without getting clearance for some of the songs, right?" Crystal converts it into her currency.

"Exactly," the lawyer says.

"Excuse me?" I butt in just to make one last thing perfectly clear. "Are the executors and the university, one and the same?"

"Yes," the lawyer says. He makes a note on his pad. And I get the feeling that I'm going to have a hard time getting any work for a while.

"What's the offer?" Crystal gets right back to it.

"You relinquish all claims to ownership of copyright. It's a one time inclusive of all rights offer. Ten thousand dollars."

"I'll think about it," Crystal Gail knows how to sing *and* dance.

"Mrs. Miller," the lawyer allows himself a little smile of satisfaction, "the late Dr. Haywood, for whatever reason, included your name on some of his early theoretical work. He gave you credit, in effect, for helping to create his work. Just how much of 'random associated pattern theory' do you remember, Mrs. Miller? The university is prepared to go to court." The lawyer sees no further point in playing nice. "Frankly, we don't believe that you can establish any claim to copyright."

"What have you found out?" Crystal has a way of getting right to it. At my age, that is a quality I admire, but still, it can be quite tiring.

"Your old boyfriend was quite the egghead," I say. "All I know is that it seems like the university wants to publish his papers. And they must be important because the university has just been offered a big whack of money for them."

"I told you Robert was something smart," she says with hometown pride.

"I went and nosed around his old department," I say. "Not everyone shares your high opinion. One of his colleagues even said that 'Haywood's work is voodoo math.' I don't get why whatever he did is such a big deal, and why it puts knots in the shorts of the other eggheads, but it does."

I haven't figured out exactly what the game is, but I'm ready to bet that Crystal is holding a big enough piece of trump to win at least one good hand. And I've got a good read on Crystal too. She's already purring, she's about to sidle over and rub her dander all over me. It's not the sort of thing that I'd encourage normally, but work has been slow and hard to come by.

"Crystal?" I'm searching for the right note to bring us to the subject of money. "I can't afford to put any more unbilled hours into this."

"You promised to help me." Her back goes instantly up, and her professionally trained voice swells with something that sounds like betrayal. Now she makes her voice very tiny, "Maybe I should just take the ten grand?"

"You don't want to do that." I hurry to her side to offer advice and comfort. "You're not going to let that bastard lawyer lowball you."

"What should I do?" Crystal asks. And I swear I can hear the sweet surrender in her voice.

"I want a third of what you get," I say.

"I'll give you fifteen percent of everything over ten thousand." Crystal has already done her math.

"Twenty-five percent of the total amount," I counter.

"Twenty percent, and we could both be happy?" She extends her hand.

I should have started off at fifty.

"Where do we begin?" Crystal is positively giddy now.

"We'll start at a place that I know you'll love," I say. "We are going to see a man who is very, very rich."

Mr. Carmello Rousseau meets with us in his games room: a pool table centers the room, there is a wall full of photos of large shocked and surprised fish, a bar at one end, and another wall of trophies. Crystal attached herself to him like a rudder, and with every quarter turn he is asked for comment or explanation — "Oh my, did you land that huge monster all by yourself? How did you win all those trophies?"

My head spins just from watching her. Rousseau seems quite willing to be led about, and Crystal shows no signs of letting go. I don't really have a plan. All I know is that Rousseau just anted up two million dollars to the university to get a hold of Dr. Haywood's unpublished papers. I figured if he'd pay that much to the university, he'd almost certainly like to own Crystal's rights to the papers too.

"Mr. Rousseau," I say, "you are interested in Dr. Haywood's work."

"He was a brilliant man." Rousseau untangles himself from Crystal. "I owe everything to him."

"Robert and I were good friends." Crystal reestablishes her hold. She's already looking to squeeze me out. "Robert was my sweetheart," she coos, "first love and all that."

I don't have a read on Mr. Carmello Rousseau; 'reclusive investor' just about covers everything that I do know. He's supposed to be some sort of stock market whiz.

"You broke his heart," Rousseau says to Crystal. "I never saw a man so heart-broken."

"Well yes, I suppose I might have," Crystal admits. She releases her grip.

Rousseau goes over to his pool table. He nudges the cue ball into place and fires it into the cluster of balls. The break is clean and the balls go flying every which way.

"Can I have a drink?" Crystal asks.

"It's open." Rousseau points at the bar. He takes the first shot. It's his table, his house, his rules.

"Everyone for Scotch?" Crystal regroups at the bar.

I wait to see what Crystal will do but she doesn't have a next move. She slinks into a chair, and now she wants me to take the point. Rousseau walks around the table; he has no shot that I can see. He sends the cue ball on a wild carom and somehow sinks one of the balls.

"Life," Rousseau smiles, "is full of randomness."

Rousseau works the table with the ease of someone who plays regularly. He has a good stroke, and it's a while before he misses. We play two quick games without saying much more than "good shot" or "tough luck," and clinking the ice in our drinks. I don't have my best stroke going, but it wouldn't have mattered.

"The university made Mrs. Miller a preliminary offer for her rights to some of Dr. Haywood's unpublished papers," I open with a neutral card.

"Yes," Rousseau says, but I can't tell if he means it as a question or an answer. We enter into a long uncomfortable silence, the kind that when you come out of it, you don't know whose turn it is.

"I took Dr. Haywood's economics class years ago," Rousseau finally says. "I went back to school to better myself. All I had was determination. I absolutely didn't get it — economics. I would stick around after class to try and get Dr. Haywood to explain it to me again. Dr. Haywood said the only way he knew how to tutor was in a pub over a pint."

That draws a bit of a laugh out of Crystal Gail. Rousseau turns and gives her a funny sort of look.

"He used to talk to you, all the time," Rousseau says. "I didn't catch on at first. I didn't know any Englishmen. I thought he was speaking *sotto voce*, but no, it was you, he spoke with *you*. He turned to you, to make his ideas into theories. And it was with you, he first argued his proofs."

"He was always an odd one, that Robert." Crystal nods in recognition. "I used to go and do my set with Billy Morris, and when I came back, Robert would still be on the same conversation, but only much further along."

I can solve the mystery now of how Crystal Gail got her name included on Dr. Haywood's papers, but I don't see where the money is. Crystal looks at Rousseau. She's about to say something; I glare at her to zip it.

"You certainly are a big fan of Robert's work," Crystal says, ignoring my warning.

"Oh yes." Rousseau is in an upbeat mood; he goes over to the bar and offers to freshen our drinks. The only play we have left is to lay down our cards.

"Mr. Rousseau," I ask, "do you have an interest in acquiring Mrs. Miller's copyright, her share of Dr. Haywood's papers?"

"I could do that, I suppose," Rousseau considers, "but I don't have to."

"Ten thousand," Crystal feels it slipping through her fingers, "that's what the university offered me."

"That's quite a bargain price," Rousseau says. "I just paid the university two million."

"What about the copyright and royalties and all that?" Crystal is still working from the lawyer's old version of the script. She's missed the rewrites. There will be no posthumous tribute, no special collection of Dr. Haywood's papers.

"What if she were to publish the papers herself?" I make one last desperate stretch. "What if she put it out on the Internet?"

"Why would I release my half of the copyright?" Rousseau chalks his cue. "And I have the only copies."

"What do I get?" Crystal's voice goes up a couple of octaves. "Don't I get anything?"

"Dr. Haywood always said that you were the source of his inspiration. He said that you gave him that very first spark. Once, after we had had a few pints, he said that something you said was the trigger for all of his work on pattern recognition."

Rousseau banks the cue ball hard along the table; it makes a diamond, and comes to rest in front of Crystal.

"I will give you 100,000 dollars, if you can tell me what Dr. Haywood meant by fifteen fingers?"

Crystal stares at the cue ball; it is solid and white, impenetrable.

Voodoo math. I went back and asked Dr. Haywood's colleagues for a better explanation. Dr. Haywood's early papers remained unpublished because they were "ridiculous and did not stand up to peer review."

I still don't get all of his theory. But there is, for example, a correlation between the lengths of women's skirts and the stock market. When short skirts are in fashion, the market rises. This is what is known as a "random associated pattern." Simple coincidence to you and me, but not to Dr. Haywood. He devised proofs — ways to identify these patterns, and also the means to predict when the patterns would most likely deviate.

Carmello Rousseau, after a brief stint at university, became an insurance salesman. And he began to dabble in the stock market. He had some initial success using Dr. Haywood's pattern recognition theories to pick stocks. I am not clear on the how, when, or why, but Rousseau decided to apply Dr. Haywood's theories to the Derivatives market. And in the arena of puts and calls, by betting for and against the future, Carmello Rousseau amassed a fortune.

Of course we went back to the lawyer. The Dr. Haywood project? Suspended. The offer to Mrs. Miller was withdrawn. The university opted to sell all of Dr. Haywood's unpublished papers to a private collector. Any concerns that Mrs. Miller might have over the disposition of the papers are to be directed elsewhere. I don't think the university ever knew what they had. Two million dollars was a small premium for Carmello Rousseau to pay for an insurance policy that kept Dr. Haywood's proofs under wraps.

⁓

"You're the brightest boy in Brighton," Dorothy Gail Lynch said.

Robert Northrop Haywood raised his head shyly to look upon an angel.

"I've read about you in the papers, and I've seen you down at the Hearthstone. I'm apt to be working there soon." Dorothy hoped that "apt" sounded smart; you wouldn't want the brightest boy in Brighton to think you are a fool.

"Billy Morris is going to let me sing with his band," Dorothy added. "I play the piano too, although not so good as my singing — not as well," Dorothy corrected herself.

"Do you like Crystal or Krystal? I'm off for a piano lesson now. You can walk me there, if you like. I swear, to play some pieces, you need fifteen fingers!"

Life in the Electronic Age

I met Larry at community college in the wake of my first marriage. He saved me from drowning in self-pity. And now it's my turn to help him pick up the pieces.

I back my pickup onto the driveway and go around to the kitchen to get the garage door unlocked. Through the curtains I can just make out four women having coffee. The coven is so engrossed in going through the entrails of Brenda and Larry's marriage that not one of them lifted even so much as a hooded eyelid my way. I'm here to clean up the after-death, to remove Larry's things from the nether world of the garage. After ten years of marriage, a man's life when measured by the cardboard boxful is not a pretty sight. Old running shoes, tennis racquets with broken strings, and mounds of correspondence, the residue of retired debts, give off a sour-sweet smell. Memories are scattered all over the house; in the kitchen they are being stamped on. The grounds of this marriage are being wrung out for the last time.

The garage has an entrance to the kitchen where Taylor, Brenda's big sister, is mining black veins of humour with a fierce relish. She keeps repeating the best of the *bon mots* aloud, trying to commit the choicest ones to memory. I request an audience with Brenda, and I'm led to the top of the stairs, where I'm instructed to wait.

So, here I am. A lone male in this hurting womb of a house, rehearsing the set speech that I have acquired for these occasions. The Bing Crosby role of father confessor and savant to the love-lorn is mine by acclamation. Two divorces and several botched relationships pass for wisdom in our suburban tribe. I'm still deciding on the right mix of concern and sincerity when I am ushered into Brenda's chamber of grief.

"Hello Brenda. I'm so sorry ——"

"Don't be. I'm not! Thanks for coming. Larry is such a shit. He can't even face me himself."

I'm trying my hardest not to stare. Brenda has turned into a beached whale. She fills the queen-sized bed like a large goldfish in a small bowl.

"My lawyer says I should let him stew for his things, but I don't want a stitch of his near my life. I feel like such an ass. There's no dignity in this, is there? I feel so ashamed, and Larry's the one who should be."

"Brenda, your life is yours again." I try for the Oprah-ized version of profound. "You can do whatever you want. You have to decide to start over, and take it from there."

"That bastard," she went on without a blink, "ten years, ten years of lies, ten years of my life flushed away!"

"Brenda? Are you all right?" Taylor comes bustling in. "What did you do?" She turns her fangs on me. "You've upset her!"

That is typical Taylor — Brenda's big sister to the rescue. Brenda is bawling like a stuck pig now. I can't get over how huge she is. Trapped somewhere inside all that flesh is the girl that I introduced to Larry when we were all at college. Brenda was in fashion merchandising, and Larry was in computer science. I was in the limbo between my first and second marriage. The three of us would drive back home on weekends. It was in the back seat of my old Mustang that their relationship blossomed, and now . . . and now it's all over.

"Carl, you have to leave!" Taylor hustles me away.

Taylor and I go back and forth in between and around our various marriages and divorces, all the way to high school. Taylor and I once had something going, underneath the cotton and elastic teenage fumbling, under the skin. Then one of those random acts that can change a life's orbit occurred. Money. A long dead and forgotten relative had left me funds with the proviso that it be spent on travel. By the time I got back . . . well it's like the man said, you can never go home. It was years before I realized that my dear dead angel never existed. It was the widowed aunt who had raised me that gave me the money. She had mortgaged her old age blanket. She never liked Taylor.

Seeing Taylor always gives me a gnawing feeling in the pit of my stomach. I go outside, and load up my truck with a random assortment of Larry's things. I boot it out to the highway. The gnawing feeling refuses to go away.

Larry has come over to my place to get his stuff. His new girlfriend, Beverley, and her kid, David, are with him. A week of bachelor living has accumulated on my kitchen table. Give Bev credit, she only wrinkles her nose once. I clear a space for us to divvy up the rest of the day.

"Mom, Mom!" David comes rushing in. "He doesn't have cable but he still gets Channel 7. How come?"

The question is really directed at Larry. It's another in a long series of tests, the prize being grudging acceptance.

"It has to do with where Carl lives," Larry answers. "The valley kind of acts like a big catcher's mitt for the TV signals. That's how come Carl can get some channels without cable."

"Oh!" David and I both say.

Point for Larry.

"I'm going into town," Bev says. "Come on David."

"Aw Mom. Can't I stay?" David pleads.

Beverley passes to Larry; he laterals to me.

"Sure," I say. "How many pounds can you lift?"

"I don't know pounds. Maybe ten kilos?" David says.

"Ten kilos. Wow! You go ahead, Beverley, we men will handle this."

"Thanks, Carl. I'll be home by five, Larry. Okay?"

Larry nods. "Take your time."

David goes into voluntary exile in front of cartoons in the den; Larry and I settle back down at the kitchen table.

"Opening time," I say.

"Hey," he grins, "I thought the rule was after twelve?"

"Only during the week," I say.

There is a special ambience that you can instantly recreate with the people you were close to in college. It's based of course on nostalgia, but there are good measures of idealism and optimism. Hovering in the kitchen are the doppelgängers of our past: two young men with lots of hair, wearing bulletin board T-shirts with cleverly ironic statements, and leather jackets with embossed letters across our backs.

Larry, ever the methodical man, uses the condensation from his beer bottle to underline slogans on a pizza box and hide his upset. He works through *Six Locations To Serve You Best* before he says, "I phoned Bren last night . . ."

"And?" I have to prompt.

He finishes *Guaranteed Hot To Your Door* before he answers.

"Taylor picked up the phone. She wouldn't let me speak to Brenda. She called me a spineless prick, and we got into a shouting match, as usual. I said she was at least half the reason why I split. She said I'd never see Tara again. I told her where to shove her broomstick — and twist. Then she said that Tara wasn't even my kid. That hurt. She said it so offhand — you know how she is. It's so ridiculous. Taylor always brings out the worst in me. She just won't let Bren and I handle this thing.

"I don't expect Bren to just forgive and forget," Larry says. "But we both know it's over. I'm just lucky that I found Bev. I wish Bren would let go."

Larry's bottle has finally run out of condensation. Out of the corner of my eye, I see David. He's been listening.

"I'm sorry, Carl — sorry. I didn't mean to come over and bring down your day. Thanks for getting my stuff."

"Sun's out," I say to change the subject. That's how Larry and I have managed to stay such good friends all these years.

If you could have asked Larry when he was a boy what he wanted to be, he would have told you, "an Indian first, or second an Astronaut." Larry grew up on the edge of some reserve land, and by Indian he simply meant one of those people from his childhood. By astronaut, Larry really meant pioneer; it was no surprise when he went into computers.

"The microchip is *the* single most important invention of our lifetime," Larry states. I should know better than to ask Larry about his job. When it comes to computers, Larry has a missionary's zeal. He preaches a sermon that lasts all the way over to Bev's house.

"Look at this typewriter," Larry says, pointing to an IBM Selectric in the garage. "When it first came out, it revolutionized typing. Now you couldn't even give it away. It's too much trouble to fix. In the electronic age, everything will be digital. It's all plug and play. If something goes wrong, you pull out the old component and plop in a new one."

"Beer me," I say.

We go inside to the den where Larry does an incantation over his computer and rigs it up for games. David is a whiz. The three of us sit transfixed; the afternoon flashes by. Bev comes home from her Saturday shopping; she insists that I stay for supper. Larry and David continue playing games on the computer; Bev and I stick to the kitchen. Bev seems so familiar. We talk until we find people that we both know and give updates. The meal turns out great. When I leave I have a nice warm buzz going. On the drive back home it finally hits me who Bev reminds me of. It was too obvious — Bren. Brenda and Larry, from when they were first married: the entire evening could've been airlifted intact from back then.

"What's all this, Larry?" I'm damn close to screaming at him.

"Peripherals," Larry says. "Think of it like buying a stereo. You've got your amp and your speakers, and now you're looking at your —"

"I know, I know, tweeters and woofers."

Larry is my gadget guru; he's given me this pet analogy before. We are in the checkout line of a big box store. On a fall Saturday afternoon, chilled by doubt, I've taken a toddling step into my life in the electronic age. I've bought a new computer. And now, even though there's a deep crater in my chequebook, I'm actually feeling relieved. I've staunched, however temporary, the growing feeling of falling further and further behind. We exit the store, and I carefully pack my brand new computer into my pickup, I can't help but think that it's got to be worth more than my old truck, and I really do not have a ready use for this electronic marvel.

"You can always rewrite the past." Larry senses my unease. "But the future only happens once."

Larry is the designated dad for the weekend. I'm Uncle Carl, his trusty sidekick. We have five kids to pick up at a roller-skating rink. Larry's daughter, Tara. David, Bev's son, And Taylor's three girls.

"Those kids must be tired of going around in circles by now," I say.

"Are you kidding," Larry says. "They love it there."

The roller-skating rink is teenage foreplay on wheels. It's late in a dance eliminator, five or six couples are left velcro'd to each other. Alana, Taylor's eldest, is among the finalists.

"She's only fourteen — barely fourteen. Taylor will kill her. And me."

"Taylor is not here." Larry restrains me. "Take it easy, don't go making a scene. Don't worry, that boy would need a crowbar to get into those jeans she's wearing."

"That boy looks like he's *got* a crowbar," I say.

Alana is finally eliminated. With the barest of nods she and her dance partner peel off in different directions. She skates over to Andrea, her sister, and Tara, Larry's daughter. The three of them convulse in giggles. Larry goes to look for David over at the video games. Heidi, Taylor's youngest, sees us and comes racing over. I've got an extra large soft spot for Heidi. She launches herself head-long at me with absolute trust. I scoop her up, and she shrieks with a delight that we should all have.

When we arrive back at Bev and Larry's, Taylor's Minivan is snub against the curb, blocking the driveway. Taylor's a realtor. She's come straight from the opening of a new subdivision with a small forest of For Sale signs in the back of her minivan.

Taylor and Bev are in the kitchen having coffee. Taylor swallows her laughter the instant Larry enters.

"Hi honey," Larry says overloud. Bev tilts her face to receive his peck.

"Mom, can David sleep-over?" Alana asks from the kitchen door.

"Go and get your sisters ready," Taylor says. "Bev, I'd love to have him."

"Are you sure?" Bev double-checks.

"I'll drop him off tomorrow on my way to my open house."

"Okay," Bev says. "You can leave the girls with me then."

"Deal." Taylor updates her Palm Pilot.

When Taylor first called me to arrange a meeting between her and Bev, I thought she was nuts. "Tara needs her father," Taylor said. "Lord knows how, but Larry is good with kids. I've done some checking up on that woman Larry lives with. Her ex-husband is in real estate. Nobody in real estate has secrets. It sounds like she's well rid of him. And it's turned into the best thing for Brenda."

I set up the meeting . . . meetings. And that's how we started up again.

Taylor and me. Me and Taylor.

"Welcome to the future." Larry salutes me with his beer.

Taylor gives us a look.

"Carl's just bought himself a new computer," Larry says.

"Oh really?" says Taylor.

I can only shrug.

"How's Bren?" Larry asks the mandatory question.

"Great. She's lost weight. Dereck's parents are flying in. I hear wedding bells." Taylor launches into a checklist of Dereck's attributes. She never stops trying out ways to annoy Larry.

We go outside. All the kids cram into Taylor's Minivan. Bev calls out last minute instructions to David to be good. Larry even comes out to the curb to wave Taylor off. He is eagerly looking forward to an evening alone.

"What are you doing later?" Taylor asks me. I shrug. "Supper's open — suit yourself." Taylor drives off. We still can't arrange even a simple thing like sharing a meal together.

I think about my new computer, about plug and play, and that old IBM typewriter. Brenda pops into my head the way she was before she got so fat. That sets me off on Taylor and my stomach acts up. I know it's ridiculous, but I feel as if I should eat. I've got that empty gnawing feeling inside.

I do a loop around the cul-de-sac. Bev and Larry's house is framed perfectly. They are in their picture window in a textbook clinch. It's like watching a scene from a movie when it comes on TV. I hold that image in my mind all the way over to Taylor's.

"Why are you being such a wallflower?" Taylor checks up on me.

"I haven't been to a party like this since our high school grad," I say.

"Isn't it great that people are finally dressing up again." Taylor sniffs, and satisfied that I'm still behaving myself, she exits the kitchen. I've got a clear line of sight into the living room. The change in Brenda is phenomenal. She didn't just lose weight: she metamorphosed. She's wearing a strapless, backless, show-it-all-off dress, and playing the gracious hostess cross-pollinating the living room. On one of her sorties she solos into the kitchen.

"Are you enjoying yourself, Carl?" She sips some Perrier with a lime wedge.

"Yeah," I salute her with my imported beer.

"You should get in there and mingle mingle." Brenda wags her finger at me. I can't help but notice. It's more pronounced now that she's lost all that weight, the resemblance between her and Bev. It's partly a bone structure thing, but it's also a style, of being of an era, coming from a background.

Dereck joins Brenda. Dereck looks familiar too. He's a better-looking version of Larry. He's an upgrade.

"Brenda and I have an important announcement," Dereck confides. He turns to Brenda. They break into a duet, "We're getting engaged!"

"Of course," says Dereck, "the marriage will have to wait until our divorces are final. But our friends are here, our parents, and tonight feels right!"

"Congratulations." I look from one set of sparking eyes to the other. "I wish you both every happiness."

That seems to do the trick. Brenda hugs me, Dereck pumps my hand, and then they start herding their guests into the basement. By the time I get there, Dereck has already made his big announcement, and he and Brenda are being thumped and smooched from all sides.

Taylor finds me at the back of the room. She insists, so we start dancing.

"What are you thinking about?" Taylor asks.

"Cars," I say.

"Thank God," Taylor says. "You're finally getting rid of that awful pickup?"

"No," I say, "I'm just thinking about old cars."

"Remember how we used to go for those long drives?" Taylor puts her head against my shoulder. "You always managed to get us lost. So we'd have to park and make out."

This is how I remember it . . . we'd keep going until we hit a crossroad. I'd always pick a secondary road and follow it for awhile, then when we came to a fork, I'd choose the one that seemed less travelled. After a bit, the blacktop would give way to gravel and then dirt. What I remember though is that we never truly got lost. One dirt road led to another, and they all eventually drained to the main highway. Taylor and I would be bumping around on those back roads for hours and then bam! We'd turn a corner and be right back where we started.

The music changes to an even slower number. Taylor's arms circle my back, one vines around my waist and the other climbs up the back of my head. I can feel the socket of her hip grate against mine. We dance in a slow tight circle.

The Other Side
of Paradise

"Come early," Bev said. "We'll eat before the hockey game. You know how Larry gets. Between hockey and playing on his computer, I hardly ever see him. We're having a few people over."

She sounded good, like one of those people who solicit for charity. "Sure," I found myself agreeing, "Saturday, sevenish, I'll be there."

After she hung up it clicked on me, the matchmaking reason behind her call. Now I'm wishing that Bev had left her call until later on in the week, to cut down on the time that I am going to spend worrying and speculating.

It's after six, bright but not sunny. A few clouds with dark bellies hang close, like back-fence neighbours talking of rain. I don't want to be too early. I take the long way around, through the city, killing time. I go past a lot of stucco post-war optimism, where siding salesmen have found their Shangri-La, past a stand of trees to where it greens into a golf course. I always have trouble finding Bev and Larry's house; there are no landmarks around here that I trust. A couple of cars are in the driveway and several others flank the house.

Just a few people, come early, Bev had said. Sure. I can see heads bobbing and hands waving. It's more a white wine than beer sort of crowd in the living room. Larry greets me at the door. I present my six-pack. He claps me on the back, clips me under his wing and circles me through a round of introductions.

I spot her right away. She's sitting on the footstool in front of Larry's easy chair. The look on her face spells relief. Mine too, I guess. Part of being single is having your married friends matchmake. This time I'm lucky; there are no visible scars. Freckles, freckles, freckles, and sandy hair to go with them, cut short at the sides and left long at the back. Green eyes heightened by a green turtleneck. She sits lotus style, in blue jeans, cradling my favourite brand of beer. When she gets up to go to the kitchen, I see that her breasts are high-up green apples. Bev's sister-in-law tags after her into the kitchen.

"Hi Carl, you ready for a beer?" Bev has flour on her hands and a smudge on her face. I can see the match-making twinkle in her eyes.

"Sure." I go to the kitchen for my beer, and a better look.

The evening quickly thins out: Roly and Mary from next door; Bev's brother and his wife; Neville — a guy who once taught Larry a computer course; Bev and Larry, Liz and me.

Neville is the gracious out, in case Liz and I don't hit it off. He's said good-bye to fifty and is within puffing distance of sixty. He has the look and smell of a confirmed bachelor: large shaggy head, smokes a pipe, wears tweed, and can talk about anything.

Larry turns coffee into an occasion by bringing out the Grand

Marnier. We toast each other self-consciously with the clink of tiny glasses. After the first period, Roly and Mary, the next-door neighbours, leave. Bev and Larry tailgate them to the door, insisting that they stay even while waving them home. In a few minutes David, Bev's son, comes home. Bev's sister-in-law digs her elbows into her husband. He insists on watching the second period. The game turns into a rout and the evening breaks up into night.

Liz and I had gotten as far as sitting on the same couch, exchanging small talk and keeping one eye on the game. She came with Bev's brother and his wife. Larry, Bev, her brother and his wife, all look at me. Liz looks at the carpet.

"Whereabouts do you live, Liz?" I ask, in what I hope is my most casual voice.

"Not very far," Bev's sister-in-law supplies.

"Near the hospital," Liz speaks up for herself. "Just the other side of Paradise."

"No problem," I say.

We both return to staring at the TV. The game is too far gone for the cameraman. He pans the crowd, zeros in on a woman in three-quarters profile, a looker. She's not interested either. She turns full face to the camera; now she's looking straight at the camera, into it. Past it. And out in a long dissolve. Beer and car commercials. Exit Neville. Bev coaches David into saying his goodnights. Liz makes herself busy with the dishwasher and putting things away. I get in her way. She hands me things to put in the fridge. Bev shadows by with a satisfied smile on her face.

We decide on coffee.

We find a neutral place. It's decorated with nuns in mind — glass all around and an antiseptic pristine sparkle inside. Puffed up waitresses in pleated uniforms are trapped behind counters full of white, sugar-dusted pastries. Fake but artful plants hang alongside cut glass lamps.

We talk about our jobs. She's a nurse. Thin ice: my ex-wife is a nurse. We skate until we find safe ground. We talk about disease.

We do so generically; we begin by cross-referencing this past winter's flu. We expand into a full-blown examination of urban hypochondria. We match every broken bone and illness that we've ever suffered. We talk and talk ourselves hungry.

French fries. More amber coffee.

A station wagon and a minivan full of square dancers bob into the parking lot. The men are in cowboy shirts with fringes. The women, young but already fat, float by. Starch crackles when they sit in pink swirls.

We talk our way from high school back to Grade One. And then up to and through nursing school and college. Stop. We skip over the '90s. The '90s is our black hole. We treat it with cold war diplomacy. When we must, we touch on it. It is our Taiwan; we still do not recognize China.

When I comment on how pale her skin is between the dots, Liz tells me how she can hardly wait for summer. We eagerly sketch out our promises for this summer. First on both of our lists is Getting in Shape. Liz talks seriously about softball. I talk tennis.

We leave with the square dancers. We watch them load the wagon and board the minivan in a well-rehearsed struggle. Through the open side of the minivan they look like huge tropical fish.

I park in front of her house; we talk some more with the windows open a crack. When we start to say good night it ends in the long foggy dissolve of a kiss. Replay.

I insist on seeing her to her door. She makes it clear, no further. We kiss again on her front steps, this time teeth and noses clash. Liz stays in her doorway waving until I reach the corner. At the lights, by the hospital, after all the talking and smooching, I realize I don't have her number, and I don't know if she's going under her maiden name, married name, or what. I'll have to get it through Bev, who will take delight in complicity.

It took me four tries to accidentally bump into Liz, marching home from work. She's taller than I remember, and older, in her nurse's uniform and the hard light of day.

"I was beginning to wonder if I'd ever find you?" I say.

Liz grins, and leads the way to a shortcut through a park. It's early April, but the park is already filled with summer: frisbees hovering like UFO guests over a family picnic, a raucous volleyball game, teenage girls in shorts and goose bumps fiercely tanning while boys prowl by on ten-speeds. Liz keeps a running tab on all the new mothers with bellies distended from a winter of fruit bearing, pushing joy bundles.

We cross the park and climb the face of a hill. The park is a billiards table below us. From deep within a concrete culvert we hear the muted roar of rushing water. Up ahead I can make out the snake of a trail under last winter's leaves, and brisk noises in the underbrush. Now the trees crowd close together, row after indivisible row of season's ticket holders. Liz sets the pace as we wind our way on and up. I begin to lag behind. She turns and fixes me with those green eyes smiling. We continue to climb but I know I am falling.

Our first dates are straight out of a high school yearbook, a movie on Fridays and dinner on Saturdays. After a couple of weeks we extend Saturday nights by returning to her place for popcorn and the late show. There was some unbuttoning but we didn't go below the belt buckle equator; we'd end up in a tangle asleep on the couch.

"Let's skip the movie," Liz says one Friday. "Softball season starts tomorrow. Come over for spaghetti. I like to load up on carbs before I pitch."

We had a really good meal; she went easy on the red wine but encouraged me. Around nine she started to stretch. I read that as a hint.

"I guess I better get going," I say.

"Please stay," she insists.

We make it past the equator, several times.

"Isn't sex before the big game too draining?" I joke.

"That's an old wives' tale," Liz says. "For men. Boxers, I think."

From then on we spend nearly every night stuck together like spoons in a drawer.

Women's softball.

At first I had my dismissive doubts, but that didn't last long. Tuesdays and Thursdays are for practice. On weekends Liz plays league. Before I knew it my weekends and my pickup were co-opted, and I became a sort of unofficial trainer and cheerleader and chauffeur. Now the back of my pickup is always filled with the paraphernalia of the game: sticky tape, unguents and ointments, shin pads, mitts, and bats. There are also other less usual items: hair barrettes, joggers bras, curiously shaped protectors, emergency supplies of sanitary pads, and specially marked envelopes for jewellery safekeeping.

Liz is a pitcher, on one hell of a team. She claims that this is her last season, and she's made an extra effort to get in tip-top shape. She wants to go out on top.

Late August is the height of the softball season. Our team is away in a tournament. We finish the round robin portion at 6 and 2 and we are in a playoff for the right to meet the home team in the final on Sunday afternoon. Injury trouble and family commitments have left us short on pitching; we're down to Baby Dobson, and our ace, Liz. In the semi-final Baby Dobson comes down with a sore shoulder. She's getting a shellacking; we have to take her out. Liz is already short on rest. If we use her now, we'll have nothing left for the final. If we don't use her, we won't be in the final. In she goes.

Liz has been our stopper all season; she's shut down this same team earlier in the tournament. This time she gets in trouble once or twice but works her way out of it. We are in the final at three o'clock.

After the game our team is bunched over by our cars. I've got the Ben-Gay out and I'm working on Baby Dobson's shoulder. One look at her face and you know why she's called Baby. Her body looks fat but I can tell you she isn't, as I work the liniment down her shoulder I can't even get a pinch on her.

Liz has an ice pack on her elbow; she's over with a dark-haired woman who has two kids may-poling around her.

"That's Joanne Long," Baby Dobson says. "She used to catch for Liz. They went to the Provincials together. Liz says she's the best catcher she's ever seen. Me too. She got married. They look kind of big but those two girls must be hers."

A few drops of rain splatter, I'm hoping that those fat clouds the sun keeps hiding behind thicken into rain. We sure could use a delay. What we get is one of those sudden summer showers, and Liz comes running over with her friend for shelter.

Joanne's kids are still out in the rain; Liz calls them over.

"Don't worry about them," Joanne says. "They love it."

The girls are playing pitch and catch; they are both very good, both left-handers, graceful and coltish. The younger girl wears a baseball cap that's too big for her and it keeps sliding down her face. The older one's hair is long and slick from the rain. We can hear their high chipmunk squeals from the batter's cage, mimicking the adults, "fire-it-in-there! Look lively!" Joanne and Liz look on real pleased.

"They're going to be ballplayers," Liz says.

"They grow so fast and change so much, it's hard to say," Joanne says. "My Randy still wants a boy. I told him, 'You think it's so easy — make one yourself. Two is enough for me.' What about you, Liz?" Joanne eyes me side-ways. "Isn't it your turn?"

"I'm working on it," Liz says.

"How's the arm?" I change the subject.

"Sore," Liz says. "But I can pitch."

The sun peeps out again. It's going to be hot for the final.

It's the largest crowd I've ever seen for softball. Players from all the other teams in the tournament are hunched and bunched along the third base line; kids and very vocal cheering husbands are drawn in like stitches against the chalk line that marks the outfield. The final is seven innings. Baby Dobson starts and she gives us two good innings. Then from the dugout we hear her shoulder pop, Liz is all the pitching we have left.

Liz's arm has no zing but we hang tough on her guile and on good defence, the score's tied going into the sixth. Then Liz starts to shoot fat Florida grapefruits and gives up a huge four-run lead into the seventh. We battle right back and give Liz a fingernail thin one-run lead to hold.

Liz walks the first batter, and the next batter hits a clean single up the middle. Runners at first and second. Liz calls her catcher over, confers with the ump, and resets her field. We know what she going to do; she's done it in practice but never in a game. She gets a new glove and will pitch left-handed. That draws a buzz from the crowd and brings out the manager from the other team.

It's a long at-bat, it goes to a full count, and Liz gets her looking at a strike. Our team goes crazy; everyone on our bench is jumping up and down laughing and hugging as if we've already won.

The next batter is no fish, and she's a lefty. She lashes a hard one-hop drive back at Liz. Cool as ever, Liz backhands the ball and starts the double play.

Game over.

There is a special riding-high feeling that you can only get in the cabin of a pickup with your lover curved next to you, and the radio playing at the fuzzy edge of the dial. I rewind an old tape, one I haven't played in a too long while: the one about getting serious, settling down, who knows?

Liz ducks out from under my wing and sits up straight.

"You don't have to promise me anything," she says. "I don't want to hear any more promises. I'm still paying off my lawyer for the last batch of promises."

Her marriage is always a dark cloud with her. I wait for the squall to pass. Liz's sniffles turn into coughs and out of the corner of my eye I see her raise her arm to wipe away tears. She gives a sharp cry of pain; she folds her sore arm carefully across her lap.

"How's the arm?" I ask.

"I've strained something for sure," Liz says.

"I bet you'll be itching to play come spring," I say.

"No," Liz says without hesitation, "that's it for me and softball."

"I can't see you quitting," I say.

"I'm pregnant." Liz stares straight ahead.

I cautiously shift the decimal point; it's a whole new equation.

"There was a time," I say while reaching for her hand, "when we would've had to get married. No question."

"There was a time, when I would've had an abortion. No question." Liz pulls away. "I didn't want to go out with you. I didn't want to do *anything* with you." I'm surprised at how angry she is.

"I thought you were just being careful." I try to lighten the mood. "An old fashioned girl."

"You're so easy to be around," Liz sighs. "I couldn't find a way to tell you that I didn't want to see you."

"That really makes me feel special," I say.

"Carl, please, please let me explain."

"Go ahead," I say. But I know that I should have been paying way more attention long before this.

"Since my divorce, most of the men I've met already have a family. They don't want to start all over again."

"I thought we had something started?"

"Carl, please. Please just let me finish."

Liz takes a deep breath; she's determined to let it all out.

"Two years ago, it got so bloody ridiculous. It's all I could think about. Those med students at the hospital are always after us nurses. I thought about picking a foreign one, in his final term. He'd never know. And the baby would have good genes. Most of the sperm banks use medical students. But I could never get the right one on the right shift, or with my ovulation cycle.

"Then you came along. I thought why not? We'd do it once or twice and then I'd break it off."

"So why did we keep doing it? Just in case your calculations were off?"

"You don't have to yell, Carl —"

"And what about the kid? Do I even get to see the kid? Did you work all of that out too?"

"Carl, the last thing I want is for you to feel like you were pressured into something you don't want —"

"I don't want you doing any more thinking for me."

"I couldn't wait any longer! I'm angry at myself," she adds, "but mostly at you."

"At me?"

"Where were you? Where were you, Carl? Five, ten years ago?"

"I was out making other mistakes!"

I am willing to continue the argument, but Liz is not.

We are poles apart in the front seat of the pickup. Our silence blurs into white lines, the passing lane, the turnoff. We coast through the city, and up to her house on Paradise. Liz takes her hurting arm inside. I unload my pickup into her garage. I empty everything out. I don't know what to think, or what to do next. I go around front; her house is in total darkness.

When I get home my phone is ringing and ringing.

Point No Point

Dennis has done all right for himself by basically doing nothing. He has a real nice piece of property out in Langford, and depending on how you look at it, Dennis' backyard is like an antique car lot or a graveyard for old junkers. He's got at least a dozen vehicles, all of which are in close to some sort of working order, but none will ever make it all the way back to what I'd consider cherry. With all the original parts he's got lying around, he could easily tidy up four or five. He could go on the Internet and get some yahoo to pay him the big bucks. Or he could package up the lot, move down to Arizona, spread his mess out like an exhibit somewhere in the desert, and call himself the curator.

Those are the sorts of things that Dennis and I talk about. I'm really quite fond of Dennis. As fond as you can be of your ex-wife's second husband.

Dennis knows why I'm here, and I know he's going to try and avoid me. He's around back in his workshop as usual, on his knees, and he has what looks like a Chevy tranny pulled apart. He's carefully trying to fit the pieces together, and he's swearing softly, as if he's learning to conjugate a verb in German.

"Let no man rent asunder that which he cannot put back together," I say, but Dennis is unwilling to get on a biblical rant with me.

"Aha!" Dennis holds two pieces up, as if he's on the Learning Channel and he's just discovered the real reason why dinosaurs went extinct.

"You'd think that somebody down at GM could have figured out a better release for this valve?" Dennis is ready to launch a tirade, and normally I would help. I would at least offer to hold the bazooka.

"It's a sunny day, Dennis," I say to remind him why I'm out here. "How do you want to work this?"

Dennis continues to putter, taking a scoop of kitty litter from a jumbo bag and spreading it over the fresh oil slick. The floor of his workshop is like a sea full of small islands of kitty litter.

"We could go in one car?" I offer. "I'll drive."

"We should take Lori's car," Dennis suggests.

"That might be an idea," I say. "Is it running?"

"It wouldn't take much to get the old wench going." Dennis warms to the idea. "I'd want to check her battery, and I'd have to switch plates."

Lori's Volvo dates back to when we were married. It was cranky even then, but reliable in a butt-ugly, solid-as-a tank way.

"Why do women like these old Volvos?" Dennis fishes for the keys.

"It's the box-y shape." I take the keys from him. We've been over this particular ground before. "And I think they must like the sound of the word — Volvo."

"Vol-vo," Dennis chuckles as he stretches it out.

"You go and get cleaned up." The trick with Dennis is to keep him moving in the right direction. "I'll have a look. Don't forget Lori," I yell after him.

Last winter, Lori made Dennis and me promise, on her dying bed, that we would spread her ashes. All she asked for was a sunny day in spring. The Lord and everyone else knows that I've broken just about every promise that I've ever made to you, Lori, but this one is the last one, and I intend to keep it.

"Do you want to stop at the Six Mile?" Dennis is an old rugby player — he has a permanent thirst. "I suppose we could," I say. I'm an old rugby player too.

It doesn't matter much which road you take, by the time you get to the Six Mile House, every idiot who's ever won their driver's license in a raffle is out playing Russian roulette in the traffic. There was a time when I could join in at just about any table at the Six Mile; the clientele still breaks down into regular regulars, long-time regulars, and all those who still "remember when all of this was Indian land."

"What did Lori say to you?" I ask Dennis when we finally get our drinks.

"Say what?" Dennis is a bit confused.

"About her ashes?" I have to shout, above the music and the TV.

"The Inner Harbour," Dennis shouts back. "Spread them in the Inner Harbour."

"Did she have a spot in mind?" I ask.

"She didn't say exactly," Dennis says, "but I figured on the spot where she used to take her lunch-time smoke."

Lori worked in Secretarial Services, at the Legislature, for years. I'm guessing the spot Dennis has in mind has to be close by, probably on the boardwalk.

"Just about every time we met up for lunch," Dennis says, "we went there. She had a game going, looking at the tourists, and trying to imagine where they were from. But with all the Japanese, that was too easy, so we went to guessing what they did for a living instead."

In all the years that I was married to Lori, I can't say that I can recall ever meeting up with her for lunch at work. We were always on different schedules.

"What do you think the most common job is?" Dennis asks.

"Dennis," I say, "I have absolutely no idea."

"Insurance and banking," Dennis states.

"Where did you get this gem, this nugget of information from, Dennis?"

"We asked them," Dennis says. "Lori and me, we conducted our own private survey of the tourist population in the Inner Harbour."

"That is totally bogus science," I say.

"Anecdotal knowledge," Dennis replies. Once he takes a position, he is prepared to defend it. "Near as I can tell," Dennis explains, "insurance and banking are a lot more rolled in together over there in Japan, as compared to here."

"Correct me if I am wrong, Dennis, but are you trying to tell me that you and Lori would walk about the Inner Harbour on her lunch break and harass the tourists?"

"We didn't always go in for tourists," Dennis confesses. "Sometimes we went after local knowledge."

"Jesus Christ, Dennis. Now you're telling me that my ex-wife and you, the pair of you, would pretend to be from someplace else?"

"It was great fun," Dennis says. "Sometimes we'd get right into our characters, accents and all, and we'd just run with it. Sometimes . . . Lori never made it back to work."

I have a jealousy flashback, as I imagine this scene of Dennis and Lori checking into a hotel in the middle of the day, without a speck of luggage. I can see the clerk at the front desk — eyes rolling.

"We should get going," I say. Dennis reaches under the table, and comes up with Lori's urn.

"Jesus Christ! Dennis! Why did you bring that in here?"

"I wasn't going to leave her all alone out in the car." Dennis shrugs. "She's been in here lots of times."

"You've got her under the table? For God's sake, Dennis, you know how Lori would feel about that."

"Keep an eye on her for me." Dennis lumbers off to the washroom.

Lori? How could you marry an oaf like that? I still resent Dennis. I still have my suspicions about exactly when the two of you got started, but if I can't pull off gracious, I can at least stick to indifferent. This is the last goodbye, and I'm not going to waste it going off on Dennis. Let's not go through all that again!

"Have you made your arrangements?" Dennis asks.

"I've always seen myself as a lie-down-in-green-pastures kind of guy," I say. "But now, Lori's got me rethinking my whole exit strategy."

"Me too," Dennis says. "My dad bought a six-pack, years ago. Out at Hatley Memorial. You know my dad; he couldn't pass up a bargain. 'Thank god, I lived to see the day when you two got married,' my dad said. Dad gave us two burial plots as wedding gifts."

"That is exactly the sort of thing I could see your dad doing," I say.

"I went out to Hatley's to see what — if anything — I could do with the extra plot," Dennis says. "Do you know that Hatley's has a whole section now just for urns? You can bury your ashes, but that seems kind of redundant."

"If I go the cremation route," I confide to Dennis as we park the Volvo, "I'd want my ashes spread in a few places."

Dennis is not open to suggestions. He surprises me by hailing a horse and buggy. I've lived here all of my life, and I've never once taken a horse and buggy. It's strictly a tourist trip. But Dennis is well into it. I can tell that this is something else he must have done with Lori. And riding high in the buggy adds a bit of pomp to the circumstance.

It's not as easy as you think, spreading someone's ashes in a place as public as the boardwalk. Tourists don't zip by you — they stroll. They are on holidays, and they will stop and smell the roses whenever they bloody well like. And they all have cameras. Do anything remotely interesting — never mind suspicious — and they will zoom in on you, like paparazzi.

"Here, hold on to Lori," Dennis says in exasperation, after several unsuccessful attempts at spreading her ashes. "I'll be right back."

I could come right out and ask Dennis, I suppose. But it's not the sort of thing you ask a man for. But if you stop and think about it, I have seniority. I was married to Lori for twice as long as Dennis.

I already have motive; I seize the opportunity. I had no intention to be greedy about it, but I end up with probably a little bit more than half. Which is fair. And besides, it's a hard thing to estimate — it's not like I had a scale with me. What I really wished I had was some sort of proper container; there's a lot more gristle and boney bits than I expected. I put what I can of Lori in my coat pockets.

"I don't know why I didn't think of this in the first place," Dennis says when he comes back. He has a bunch of tickets in his hand and he's all smiles. There's a little putt-putt taxi ferry that leaves from the Wax Museum and criss-crosses the Inner Harbour over to a marina in Esquimalt. Dennis has bought all the tickets.

"Come on, Lori," Dennis says as he takes the urn, "we're going for a boat ride."

It went pretty smoothly after that, on the boat. Once we got the wind direction sorted out.

"You did it up right." I give Dennis a thumbs up. We're back at his house.

"Do you know that it's against the law to bury human remains on your own property?" Dennis asks.

"I didn't make the law," Dennis adds. "I'm just letting you know it's on the books."

Dennis is on to me. It wouldn't take much to jumpstart an argument. But we both decide to let it idle. It doesn't seem like the time or the place. We shake hands; somewhere down the road there'll be a rematch.

The place I have in mind is actually not all that far. Once you are out in Langford, Sooke is not all that much further, and once you're on the way to Sooke, the drive takes over. If you don't slow down on the road to Sooke, you're a danger to yourself and to others, and a bloody idiot for missing out on some of God's best stuff. You've got sea and sky, mountains and coastline, and you've got your rainforest.

The problem is, I can think of at least a dozen places between Sooke and Renfrew. I remember one time at Sombrio when I watched you watch a starfish in a tidal pool for an hour. That was a perfectly glorious day. I know you asked for a sunny day, Lori, but I keep remembering those rainy nights when we went camping, and how we both managed to fit like two fingers in that old glove of a sleeping bag, which I still have.

Here we are. It's that beach we used to go to back in high school — the one near Point No Point. We stopped coming here after we got married, I don't know why, but it always seemed like a place for teenagers. Do you remember the week before our grad? You were with Doug Richards — the Rooster. His claim to fame was a Pontiac Bonneville and a lick of hair that wouldn't stay down. And I was with Razor, who never got asked for ID, and she always got the booze for us. No one knows what became of Razor, and I'll bet the Rooster is still mad at you. When you broke up with him just before grad, he had to go with his little sister.

The way I remember it, a bunch of us had a bonfire going on the beach, and we were planning a huge prank for grad. We were going to leave a mark for everyone to see. We wanted to get our stories straight. And we were drinking ourselves sillier than usual.

This is it. About here, with the crash of waves and the sucking sound of gravel straining through the undertow, just like this. I've never pretended to understand poetry, and I don't remember now if the sky was a basket of stars, or if the moon was wrapped in a blanket of cloud. It's as close as I can get. This is where we stood shivering and taking urgent turns hurling into the ocean, and swearing to sweet Jesus that we would never ever drink, never again! God, how I wish I had stuck to that one promise.

Do you think I've chosen the most unromantic moment possible? Lori, I think it was the most honest, the purest moment in our lives. In my life anyway. We stood here talking for God knows how long. About finally finishing high school, about looking for jobs, about all that and everything. We had our hopes. The future was as big as the ocean in front of us.

"What should we do?" I said. I meant about returning to the others.

"We should leave only footprints," you said. I've always remembered that. You must've got that from somewhere, Lori. But it was the first time I ever heard anybody say something so perfect as that. And that was the start of us. As for the rest of it, I've never asked for a discount on blame, and I'll admit to nothing more than what you don't already know. The hardest part of saying goodbye is knowing that what we had was already gone.

When All Love Was Lost

"Poor Lois was mortified," my wife said. "Lois is at the end of her rope with Marty."

"Let me try and talk to him," I offered.

My wife gave me that look that she's got perfected: you go and do what you have to do, and then we'll do it my way. My wife met Lois years ago, down at St. Jude's. Lois was looking to bail out from her job as a psych nurse. St. Jude's didn't want to lose her, so they found a spot in the records department. That's where my wife works; she's in the records management end at the hospital. My wife has worked her way quite nicely up the ladder at St. Jude's. Whenever there's a big to-do she is always on the committee that plans the festivities. At the last shindig, Marty — Lois's husband — was way over the top. There is a point where commonsense is supposed to kick in, where you say all right good night sayonara adios. Marty's off button was busted; that switch on his console was broken.

The big thing that we have in common with Lois and Marty is that we each have two kids, and our kids are close in age. Another thing is that me and Marty, we are both in the same trade. Marty is a pretty fair electrician. He works for building services at the university. And I do pretty much the same for the works department with the city.

We used to share the rental on a cottage for two weeks in the summer. One couple would go up and get things set up, and the other couple would pack up and close it down. When we got to know them better, one couple would take all four kids, and each couple got two days to themselves. It was a pretty fair arrangement, and it lasted for a few years until the kids got to that point where doing anything with their parents was lame.

A couple of years back, when the university was talking layoffs and the city was talking buyouts, Marty and me put some serious thought into going into business together. We kicked around several ideas, and we ended up trying to get into the home security business, installing alarms. I saw it more like selling a service. Marty saw it as selling a product. He went ahead and purchased a butt-load of alarms. I did my best to help him unload them, but one wall of his garage is still stacked from floor to ceiling with house alarms.

"What's up?" Marty was surprised to see me. The thing is, once we get past giving updates on the kids and wondering what the wives have in store, there's not much to talk about. I'd have to say that it started to get like this even before we ventured into business.

"How's Leon?" I asked about his older boy.

"He wants to be called Leo now," Marty said. "He's moved out. He's living with a girl. And she thinks Leo is cool. As soon as they start getting their whistle wet on a regular basis there's nothing more you can say to them."

"At least one of yours is out the door," I said. "Mine show no signs of leaving, and why should they? The way we coddle them."

Marty offered me a beer, and I think about turning it down in light of what I've come to talk to him about. But it's no use starting off on a high horse. That's not going to sit right with Marty, so I accept the beer.

"You were pretty well plastered, the other night," I ventured.

"I don't remember much." Marty shrugged.

"What's up with that?" I said.

"Lois put you up to this?" Marty's on the red line, he's on defence.

"Lois hasn't said a word to me." I tried to back him off a bit. "Your wife didn't put me up to anything. That job is already taken. My wife is the one who put me on your tail. We're both of us concerned."

"I didn't pace myself right," Marty sidesteps. "Those people down at the hospital, all they talk about is how management is looking to screw them, and the latest mystery disease that's going around. It's a bloody miracle we aren't all dead already."

We sip our beers. I gave it a minute before I start up again.

"Either you can't hold your liquor anymore or you're drinking way more than your fair share. I've seen you crash hard, but not like that. That was a total wipe out."

Marty just stood there at his workbench, not saying anything. And now I'm thinking, maybe this is not such a good idea? Marty's troubles are his own business. I'll finish my beer, and leave the man be.

"You met my dad? When he was out here, didn't you?" Marty asked.

"Yeah." I'm trying to recall the one time when I met his dad, a year or so back. I remember being introduced and thinking that the apple didn't fall far from the tree.

"He passed, recently," Marty said. "I'm the same age now that my dad was when he left my mom."

I have a fair idea what's bugging Marty now. And I don't know how to respond to that. But I do know what I'll say to my wife. I'll tell her that Lois may have herself a much bigger problem on her hands than she realizes.

"When I was thirteen my mom and dad split up. Me and my dad went to live in a big apartment complex. I was pretty pissed with my dad for uprooting me. It was winter, I had to change schools, and I didn't know anybody at my new school. My dad was a stonemason. You know what that trade is like — too much work in the summer and none at all in the winter. My dad did odd jobs around the complex. The building manager was a guy named Bob Rennie. He and my dad went back a ways. Most of the time they sat around drinking and reliving the good old days, but at the end of the month when people were moving in and out they had to go like stink.

"My dad had himself a girlfriend," Marty said. "Her name was Marika, but my dad hardly ever called her by her name. He did that with everybody. With me it was 'hey partner,' or 'come on sport.' My mom was always 'the wife,' or 'the missus,' even to her face. That's one of the things that drove her crazy. He called Marika 'my pet,' or 'here's my girl.' I don't know if it upset her. She didn't let on if it did.

"Right after the girlfriend moved in with us, she shaved her head. She was bald. I mean completely bald. Every couple of days she'd scrape off the little bit of peach fuzz, and then she would oil that thing up. I used to watch her do it. She didn't mind me watching. And I was at that age where I was starting to get ideas.

"My dad was always buggering off somewhere with his pal Bob Rennie, and leaving me alone in the apartment with her. She used to tell me what it was like for her as a kid, and how she came to Canada from some god-forsaken place. I don't remember much more than that, I was too busy being angry at my dad. I took it out by yelling and screaming at her. She'd turn on the waterworks, and that shut me up. It didn't stop me from being angry, but it shut me up.

"She used to call me, 'her little big man.' I'd come home from school and she'd fix me up a snack. Sometimes she'd make the full meal deal, and we'd wait around for my dad to show. But if he was late, or if he just plain forgot, she didn't make me wait. And she didn't care if I ate right in front of the TV.

"She would come and go; she'd disappear for weeks at a time. The whole setup didn't last all that long, less than a year. After a while my dad and me moved back in with my mom. That didn't last long either; the old bastard was gone for good before too long.

"I didn't see him for years. I knew he'd go downhill. But when he came out last year, it was still a shock to see how far. It was Lois's idea. I knew he came looking to make peace before the buzzer," Marty said, "but there was nothing left to say."

It hits me that I don't know all that much about Marty, before kids. Neither one of us is big on the good old days. We don't go on and on about stuff like that. There's the occasional flash from the past, like when I met his dad, but maybe you can never really know how much of someone's present is tied up in their past. At least I have some idea now about what's eating Marty. I'll pass it along to Lois and maybe she can work with that, cut him some slack, give him some time to sort himself out. I don't know what else she can do.

"Did you know that Marty's dad just passed?" I asked.

"Of course," my wife said, as if this was common knowledge and it's only the village idiot who doesn't know. I don't know what she's so upset about? She's been operating on a short fuse; it's like she wants this thing between Marty and Lois to blow up. My wife doesn't care for Marty. She is friends with Lois, and she is friends with Lois and Marty. My wife has a way of putting things into compartments. Maybe that stems from her job in records management? Or maybe that's why she has a job like that?

"Lois wants to leave him. Don't act so surprised. It's been coming for a long time. Lois is coming by to discuss the situation. Make sure and tell Lois everything that Marty told you."

I'm more than sure that she and Lois have already "discussed the situation," and a course of action has already been decided. Marty is in for it.

I really like Lois. The first year we rented the cottage, Marty couldn't get away for the first week, and Lois and the kids came on ahead with us. One morning we took all the kids and let Lois sleep in. Later on I went back to the cottage for something; I walked in on Lois just as she was stepping out of the shower. She didn't go eek! or run for cover. And I didn't peek and turn away. She stood there slowly towelling herself off, all nice and natural. I took a good long hard look. And she looked right back at me.

That look has stayed with me. It was about sex and desire, and all of that. But it was something more too. It felt like I had been let in on the last secret, and that I was somehow, finally, a full-grown adult. I still carry around that naked Lois, and I draw her out once in a while. At the St. Jude's Christmas party, we have a slow dance or two. We meet up for coffee; we go for walks. It's not about sneaking something past our spouses; it's our way of acknowledging that we are alive in the world, and that there is still the possibility of a life outside of the one that you're in.

Lois and me, we talk about things that I'm pretty sure she doesn't talk about with my wife. For instance I know why she was transferred into the Records Department years ago; she crossed the line with a patient, she got too involved. It happens more than you'd think. She's told me stories about working on the psych ward, and how a nurse can get so wrapped up in the life of a patient that they'd pee in a juice jar to give someone a clean urine sample. Lois's battery has run right down from time to time, but she's always been able to recharge and get back at it.

"I had a talk with Marty," I told Lois when she arrived. "He said that Leon's out the door. Leon's living with a girl now."

"Is that what he told you?" Lois said. "Leon and Marty had a huge fight. Leon couldn't stand to be around him anymore and moved out."

"I'm sorry to hear that," I said.

"I've been after Marty for years: go and see a counsellor, get some help. There's no shame in getting help when you need it.

I've tried to help him, but I've only made things worse. I tried to get him to reconcile with his dad before it was too late. I got in touch with his dad and invited him out. I hoped that he and Marty could put some things to rest. But it didn't work out. Marty just got worse and worse after his dad left."

"He did talk about his dad a little bit," I volunteered. "He didn't say much, he told me about when his mom and dad first separated, and how he went to live with his dad in an apartment. He mentioned a woman named Marika. He said she was bald."

"Did he say who she was?" Lois asked.

"He said she was his dad's girlfriend."

"Marty," Lois said, shaking her head, "is so deep in denial. He can't even bring himself to admit to the simple truth. Marika was his mom. His birth mom. She gave him up. Her older sister looked after Marty right from birth.

"The aunt who raised Marty had made her sister swear that she would never tell Marty who his real mom was. That was the price she extracted at the start, and she was determined to make his birth mom stick to it. After thirteen years, Marika decided she wanted to claim her son.

"Marty's dad told me there was a huge argument between the sisters, and all love was lost. Marty's dad took it upon himself to play Solomon; he took Marty away to live in an apartment with his birth mom.

"Marika had her full share of troubles. She was sick. Cancer and chemo — that's why she was bald. She wanted to spend some time with Marty, before she died.

"I see people like Marty at work everyday," Lois said. "I don't want to have to come home to that too."

"What do you want me to do?" I asked.

"I'm planning an intervention," Lois explained.

"How does this intervention thing work?"

"It's a show of support," Lois said. "We set up a time so people can come by and let Marty know that they care. He'll see that he has a network he can call on."

The support that Lois is after is as much for her as for Marty. At

the end of the day, Lois wants everyone to know she did everything she could; she reached out to his family and his friends, the
community. If she's going to leave him, it won't be long now.

"I'll bounce it off some people that me and Marty know in common," I offered. "Is there's a time that's good or better for Marty?"

Lois pulled out her pocket calendar. She's ready to pencil in
Marty's intervention. Was there ever a time when it was good or
better for Marty?

Lois and my wife have read up on interventions. They have access
to all sorts of material through St. Jude's. They have it broken
down into disease and illness. Some people have a disease; there
are symptoms and there's treatment. A disease either has a cure
or not. Other people have an illness. They are sick. Lois doesn't
believe in cures when it comes to mental illness. What you have
are causes and outcomes. The cause of a mental illness is usually
one or more of three things: guilt, shame, or regret. Marty's got
the trifecter. He's in a bind, he can't get a grip, and he can't let
go. Marty won't have a positive outcome.

I got to play Marty in the dress rehearsal for the intervention.
It's a tough role. I swear my wife was doing more than just a practice intervention on me. It gets very personal, very fast. I seriously doubt that this is going to work with Marty. His fuse is a lot
shorter than mine.

The intervention is in an hour. I don't think Marty has a clue;
he thinks Lois is putting on a spread for Leon and his girlfriend,
as a welcome to the family. I'm supposed to keep Marty in check
until the face-off.

When I arrive, Marty is in charge of the barbeque, as always.
Marty is old school; he's a charcoal man. He swears by it. You can
argue about the time it takes, but not the results. My wife and Lois
are in the kitchen making comfort food. They are cooking up a
storm.

"What are you going to do with all these alarms?" I ask.

"I still sell a few, here and there," Marty lies.

"They make excellent Christmas gifts," I reprise a line from our sales pitch.

"Can you truly put a price on peace of mind?" Marty adds another line. "And you get free installation from a certified electrician."

"I still think you should turn that around," I say, offering my usual solution. "Sell the alarms at cost or below, but charge an hourly rate for the installation. Throw in some kind of an inspection. Fiddle with the fuse box. Walk around with a stud finder, make some beep beep noises, have a cup of tea, and there's your hour."

"When you're right, you're right. But that still don't make it right." Marty cracks another beer.

"I need something solid in my stomach first," I beg off.

"I've got smokies," Marty suggests. "Bavarian with cheddar."

"Do you still have any of that Cajun hot sauce?" I ask.

Marty went inside to check. I do a spot count on the empties; he's already had a few. A couple more and this intervention will go from a drill to a riot. Marty comes back with a plateful of smokies. I don't know if somebody said something to upset him, but now he's turtleing. My wife will have my head if Marty tanks now. It'll ruin the whole evening she and Lois have planned. I can't stomach the idea of marching him into a room full of people, good intentions and all, like he's some kind of piñata for everybody to take a whack at.

"You've got Lois worried shitless," I say. "Lois thinks it has to do with your dad passing. She said what you're going through is called 'delayed grief onset.' And your dad's passing was a trigger that released something deeper. Lois thinks it goes back to when you and your dad went to live with Marika?

"Marika was your mom." I put that out on the table too.

Marty goes over to the grill to flip the smokies. He's in full lockdown mode.

"My dad was such a bastard," Marty finally says. "He stuck the two of us together in that apartment. I was thirteen years old. Alone in an apartment with a woman. She was a lot younger than my dad. I kept trying to look down her shirt to see her nipples. I walked in on her in the bath. I wanted to fuck her. I thought about it constantly. I imagined us doing it. I didn't know! Why didn't he tell me? Why the hell didn't he tell me?"

I see where the guilt and shame enter into it. And I don't know what to say to that. I'm thinking it's time to call Lois; she's the professional. But I know where Lois stands, and right now I'm not sure she'd be the best help for Marty. The way I understand it, the intervention is supposed to be a starting point, but Marty has skipped ahead. A room full of well-meaning people, most of whom are Lois's friends, confronting him about his drinking — that just reeks of disaster.

"I knew she was my mom," Marty admits. "They never came right out and said so, but somewhere along the line I figured it out.

"I wish I had paid more attention to her. She tried to spend some time with me. She tried to tell me some stuff about herself, about who she was and where she came from. 'We've had our share of sinners and saints. We've got gypsy blood.' I remember her saying things like that. My mom, my other mom never talked about stuff like that. She hated her past. She said she was glad to leave all of that behind when she came to Canada."

Marty gets all choked up and he starts to cry. It's a hard thing to watch, and all of that rehearsal stuff we did for the intervention sounds like so much feel-good bullshit now.

"I think I can kind of see it from your dad's angle," I say. "He was in a pickle. There was no way he could please both women. How could he deny your dying mom? And how could he take you away from the woman who raised you as her own? It seems to me that your dad tried to do one nice thing for her, and for you. He gave you the chance to get to know one another."

I have no idea if this is of any comfort, but Marty seems to give it some serious consideration. And just when I'm starting to think that he's gone down his private road to his personal hell, all of a sudden he does a turn around.

"Did I tell you my dad was a stonemason?" Marty asks. "When he was out here the only thing that we could talk about was redoing the patio. He gave me some tips. He had some ideas. He always had an eye. He could size up a job. I know the drinking got in his way, but when he set himself to working on a project, he could go like stink.

"He and his pal Bob Rennie, they had the contract to redo the whole courtyard for the apartment complex where we lived for a while. There was a fountain, and a wading pool with terraced steps, the works. My dad did most of it; he worked on it bit by bit. He put it aside in the worst of the winter. He said you should never lay stone when the ground was frozen, that it didn't settle right. We would watch him from the balcony. Me and Marika. We would wave at him, but most of the time he didn't see us. He was too busy. He looked just like a giant ant scurrying around with those coloured pieces of tile.

"Marika was coming and going a lot more. She never talked about it. But by then I knew she went away for treatments, and that the treatments only made her feel worse.

"Spring was trying to make up its mind, and there was a stretch of good weather. My dad went at it hard trying to finish. The day my dad finished the courtyard, he took us out to the balcony to look down at his handiwork. He said he had a secret to show us, and you could only see it from high above, like from where we lived. And even then you had to be told how to look.

"There was a keystone. You had to find that first, and then you followed it along. You connected the dots until it formed a letter, first an M, then and A, then R. The next letter was both a T and an I, depending on how you looked at it. That took you up to the fountain, along one side was Y, and the K A on the other.

"Marika and Marty. When she realized what he had done, she jumped up and down. She clapped her hands and she hugged him and me so tight.

"Not long after that she went away. And I never saw her again. We moved back in with my mom, my other mom. Soon after that, my dad split.

"It was Lois who had the bright idea to bring him out here. It was the first and only time he ever met his grandkids. I could see that he was grateful for that.

"Before he left, I asked him about Marika. I just wanted to know something about her, about him and her. The old bastard refused to say a word. Not one word."

People are starting to arrive for the intervention. I don't know if there is any way to call a halt at this stage. Lois and my wife have too much invested. Marty is starting to catch on that something is up.

"So the last memory you have of her is the balcony? That day out there on the balcony." Marty nods. I'd thank the old bastard for that, I want to say. But I don't. Lois and my wife give the signal; it's time to bring Marty in.

"I don't know much about being a stonemason," I say. "But when you're ready to start work on your patio, give me a call."

Is There Someone You Can Call?

Today's the day. We take possession at noon. Officially.

Actually we only saw the house twice: first at the open house, and the second time was when we came out to put in our offer. We had it narrowed down. It's a little further out than ideal, but it had everything else on our wish list. We came in a little bit light on our offer expecting to be countered, but it was accepted. It just goes to show, our agent said, you never know.

It's after one o'clock, and any minute now a five-ton truck will show up with all our stuff. The problem is all the stuff from the previous owners is still here. Our new kitchen cupboards are full of their dishes. They've got the exact same set of Langostina pots, and they have the Kronvik dining room table from IKEA; we

thought about buying that, but we went with the Pelto. The clos-
ets in the master bedroom are full of his suits and her dresses, like
an orderly crowd waiting their turn to get out. The *en suite* bathroom is stocked with towels, toilet paper and toothpaste. There is
no sign of packing up. The only room that is even remotely close
to empty is a spare bedroom.

I phone my wife to bring her up to speed. "There's been some
sort of a mix-up," I say.

"Are you sure you're at the right house? Did you check the
address? The numbers?" she asks.

"Of course," I say. But she's already put me on hold. She's gone
to double-check. I know it's the right house. I've checked the
address at least half a dozen times. I've even gone all the way back
out to the highway and taken the turnoff again, twice.

My wife comes back on the line, the purchase agreement and
the title transfer are right in front of her. "Today is the day. Noon.
We take possession."

"What about their stuff?" I ask. "What's that called? What does
it say about that? The chattels?"

My wife knows a lot more about legal terms than I do.

"There's nothing in here," she says, "except for the drapes. We
asked for those. Are the drapes still there?"

"Everything," I say, "is still here."

"I can't do anything from here," she says. "Can't you handle
this?"

"I'm sure it's just a simple screwup," I say. "Their movers must
have got the date wrong. I'll put a call in to our agent. Maybe our
agent can get a hold of their agent and figure this thing out? I'll
call you back, okay? okay?" She's already hung up.

Their agent sounds like someone whose cheque has cleared;
the problem is mine. The company my wife works for is paying for
our entire move. All I had to do was show up, open the door, and
the movers would do the rest. Somehow the blame for this mix-up
will end up as mine for all eternity.

The kitchen leads into the garage. The double garage is what clinched it for me. It's Black & Decker all the way, and each tool has its own stencilled place along the walls. There's a Mazda mini-van in one of the bays. We looked at buying one of those, but we decided to wait and put the money into buying more house. It takes a minute to find the switch that controls the garage door. It's got a neat feature: you can open one side at a time or both sides at once. I come around to the front of the house again. This time, I will turn the key, open the door, and presto! House empty! You are such a child, my wife would say if she were here. You can't just wish for things to go away.

                             ~

"For a second, I thought you were Ross," the neighbour says. "I've got his leaf-blower. I didn't get a chance to return it."

The neighbour's name is Barry. He is very tall, and he's very bald. In fact Barry is too bald; he lacks the gravitas a truly bald man needs to carry off such an expanse of skin. It will take years for him to grow into that much baldness.

"It's the new, new neighbour," Barry calls to his wife.

"What does he want?" she says.

The layout of their house is the same. I hear her, but I don't see her. I'm guessing master bedroom.

"Tell her I want a cup of sugar," I say.

"He says he wants a cup of sugar," Barry plays along.

"Sugar?" His wife hesitates. "We have lots of sugar."

"I need to borrow your garage," I say.

"And he needs to borrow our garage."

Barry's wife comes to the door; her name is Cynthia. She is wearing a tracksuit and her face is flushed, as if she's been work-ing out or something.

"Don't you think he kind of looks like Ross?" Barry asks. Cynthia agrees.

"I need to borrow your garage," I say. "Unless you know how I can reach your former neighbours in a big hurry? There's a mix-up with the movers. Nothing of theirs is packed up. And our stuff will be here any minute. I can't even use the garage. A Mazda takes up half the space, and it's like a hardware store in there."

"Ross liked his tools and his toys," Barry says. "He was a handy kind of guy."

"Do you have a number for them?" I ask.

"We have no idea how to reach them." Barry confirms this with Cynthia.

"People come and go, all the time." Barry shakes his head. "I'm not saying they had an obligation, but common courtesy. We weren't neighbours for long, but we weren't complete strangers, to leave without a word — it's too weird."

"Barry?" Cynthia says. "Barry, can I see you in the kitchen for a sec?"

I recognize Cynthia's tone. Any man who's been married for a while knows that particular tone. Cynthia tries to keep her voice down. I don't know exactly what she's saying, but I get her drift. Don't get started, and don't get us involved. I'm at their door long enough to start to feel uncomfortable when Barry arrives, back-checking all the way.

"Maybe I'll hold on to the leaf-blower," Barry says.

I decide to walk down to the mailbox. It gives me something semi-useful to do. It's snowing. It's at the point where it's sticking to the lawns but not the road. I feel like I'm inside a diorama that's just been given a shake. It's a lightly frosted winter pastoral scene. This whole area used to be farmland: quietly rusting tractors still sit in weathered barns, and there's a stand of trees — a windbreak for the original farmhouse — that now acts like a divider between the new subdivision and the highway.

When my wife got the promotion and transfer, it was a big jump ahead for her, and not much was happening for me. I went to university here, so I already know my way around. That's a plus. I might still know a few people. In my last year at university, the girl I was living with had a chance to go on a work-study for a year. We didn't make any promises. I don't even know if she ever made it back. I'd like to know how things turned out. I ought to look her up. Give her a call.

The mailboxes are in a cluster near the turnoff from the highway, and there's a bit of a crowd: three trucks and a couple of cars. I can make out the word SHERIFF on one of the cars, and someone is handing out orange fluorescent vests. About eight or nine guys are forming up into what looks like a posse. A banjo music soundtrack runs through my head, and I begin to make all sorts of loose jangling connections between our new house with too much furniture and missing persons.

"Deer can't read." The sheriff points in my general direction with his rifle. "They migrate along this corridor, every year."

"Looks like you're here to teach them quite a lesson," I say.

"The deer were here first," the sheriff says. "Where's the lesson in that?"

"Look at it coming down," I say. "It must be good and thick in the mountains."

The sheriff nods as the hunters begin to fan out. I collect an armload of flyers from the mailbox and sort them directly into the recycle bin. On the way back I stay on the road, trying hard not to leave any tracks.

The movers arrive. They do what movers do when faced with any problem: they have a smoke. The driver's name is Harold, and his two boys are Colby and Rob.

Colby, for reasons known only to him, counts and recounts the extra blankets that they use to cover and slide things around. Rob is looking for a mathematical solution: if X is the volume of the moving van, and Y is the available area in the garage, then . . . Rob is unable to subtract enough information to make a clear deduction.

"You don't have a key for the Mazda?" Harold feels around under the bumper. Believe it or not, he's come across similar situations. "These things have a way of working out," Harold assures me. Now he stands on the bumper of the Mazda, and jumps up and down. "We could tow the Mazda out," Harold suggests, "without too much trouble."

"That would work." Rob's main job is to agree with Harold. Colby does another recount of the blankets.

"What about the stuff inside?" I ask. "Is there something we are supposed to do?"

"What do you mean?" Harold asks. He's immediately suspicious.

"Could you pack it up, legally?" I ask.

Harold is not at all concerned about the legal issues surrounding the stuff inside. And he has no interest in packing anything up; his obligation ends as soon as our stuff is unloaded. Harold studies the falling snow, anxious to get started. He didn't plan on this weather, and he wants to get going before dark. Rob and Colby vigorously agree.

Barry's garage yawns opens, and he emerges wearing some kind of uniform. I'm guessing that he's some sort of pilot.

"Me and Ross — we talked lawns and golf. Ross was a regular guy. I know he did some work overseas, right out of university. That's where they met. Rita was the arty type. She kept busy, seemed happy. Apparently Rita just up and left him. Poor Ross." Barry shrugs as he gets into his car. That's the full extent of what he knows. Cynthia watches from her bay window. As soon as she sees me looking she turns her back.

I find a spare key for the Mazda in the kitchen. Harold and his boys unload the truck like a military operation: the only casualty suffered is a lamp that I took from my parents' home. It went with me off to college, it survived the swamp of dorm rooms and bachelor foxholes, it sat on my night table in my only other serious attempt at setting up a nest, and it went straight into storage with all the rest of my things when we started living together.

Colby broke it. Rob calls Colby a loser. Colby hangs his head in shame. Harold says there's no need for that, and that there's a procedure for accidents. There is a form to fill out. Harold insists that I place some sort of value on the lamp. It's not *the* magic lamp, I say. It's too small a thing to make any sort of a fuss about. It probably would have just stayed in a box, until some garage sale in the future.

Harold and his boys turn down my offer of a drink; they are intent on beating the weather. The crescent retakes the contours of a farmer's field. The windbreak of trees on the near horizon stands in close for the forest that once was. The sheriff and his men are still trolling the neighbourhood, reluctant to abandon their annual hunt. How can they see in this weather? The Mazda is already covered by a coat of heavy snow. How long before it becomes a target? If I stay outside, I'll be game soon. But I'm reluctant to re-enter the house; I have this foolish feeling — not quite like I'm intruding, but as if I'm stepping on something.

"There's been a horrible accident on the highway; a truck over-turned." Cynthia comes over to inform me. She is one of those people who can make everything sound like an accusation.

"The sheriff is telling everyone not to go out. The road is going to be closed for quite a while. It's one of the charms of living out here. Barry made it through; he's ahead of the storm."

Cynthia plays the good neighbour, but curiosity is what really dragged her over.

"Come in, come in," I say. "Ignore the chaos. I found some wine. I'm assuming they won't mind. Be careful, the movers broke a lamp. I think I got it all, but watch where you step."

Cynthia can't resist taking the tour, walking through the house, and stopping in every room to take inventory.

"Is anything missing?" I ask.

"Nothing that I ever saw," Cynthia says.

Cynthia doesn't know all that much about Ross, but she fills me in on Rita. It turns out Rita went to the same university as I did. We overlapped. I might even know her to see her. When she was at university, Rita was seeing a guy named Edward for a while. Edward wasn't a student but he was always on campus. He was with some company that did a lot of business with the university. He was also attached to someone else. Rita didn't like the arrangement, but she had no one that she could call on for advice. Finally, she decided to take her student loan and go off to Mexico to sort things out.

When she got to Mexico, Rita sent Edward a postcard; it had a picture of a famous ruin. Rita spent a long time deciding what to put on the card, but in the end she went with her first thought.

I am here. You are not.

Mexico was not far enough away for her purposes, and Rita continued south. She would accept rides to anywhere from strangers, but she had surprisingly few adventures or mishaps. She went wherever people's lives were taking them, and most people were going nowhere special.

Rita met Ross in Belize. It was a case of mistaken identity. The driver who picked her up was sent to fetch a young woman from Canada and bring her to the compound where a group of well-intentioned young people were trying to make a difference. They had a project underway, and Ross was in charge. It was only for a brief time, but Rita had to pretend that she was this other woman — the no-show. Rita would sometimes think that she had somehow stepped into this other woman's life.

Ross and Rita returned to Canada. They looked at several houses before they bought. The house was a little further out of town than cither Ross or Rita would have liked, but it had everything else you could wish for. You could see deer — right in the backyard. They decided to have a housewarming party.

Edward turned up at the party.

Rita was in the kitchen with her new neighbour, Cynthia; they had made all this Mexican food.

Here you are, Edward said.

Cynthia takes her leave. I follow her tracks across both lawns. She stops and stares into the bay window of her house for a long moment before she goes inside.

It's dark and getting darker. Just as I decide to call my wife, she phones.

"Where are you?" I ask.

"Still at work," she answers.

"There's been an accident on the highway. They've closed the road," I say.

"Good," my wife says. She's not planning on driving out in this. She'll stay and work late. She'll stay in the corporate suite; no one is using it, so why not?

"How did the move go? Is all of our stuff in the house?" she asks.

"I'm not sure," I say, "about a lot of stuff."

"I labelled all of my boxes," she says. "The movers were supposed to unload everything into the right rooms. That was our agreement. They won't get paid until it gets done right. They'll have to come back. They'll have to get it right."

"There's a deer in our backyard," I say. "A big one."

"Really? What are we supposed to do about that?" she says. "Is there someone you can call?"

The Life We Had

My father's workday often spilled over into the evening, and it was not unusual for his clients to come around to our house to solicit his advice. Mr. Hadeed owned a factory that made automobile parts, mainly for export. He always had some papers for my father to look over, and he was usually accompanied by his two sons.

Greg, the older son, was a string bean, even though he was all mouth and ate as if food were going out of style. Kevin was a lot shorter and root-bound, like a plant in a too-small pot. He had recently returned from college with a head full of ideas, and he was intent on modernizing the factory. The nuts and bolts of pay-roll and personnel were left to Greg. This division of labour was not something that Greg agreed to or wanted. He and Kevin never saw things eye to eye, but there was room in Mr. Hadeed's vision for both his sons, and he still held out hope that they would come around and build together on what he had started.

Greg always had a joke or some funny story to relate. Kevin was the serious one, and even though his father understood English perfectly well, he insisted on repeating and re-phrasing whatever advice or instructions my father imparted. As soon as the business was concluded, Kevin, who was newly married, would excuse himself and head for home. Greg, who was still single and living with his parents, was never in any hurry to leave (my aunt Lydia, who was living with us at the time, had everything to do with that).

When you became involved with a girl, you dated her, but you were engaged to her entire family. Greg and my aunt Lydia never got to the serious stage. They continued to date in part because everyone so obviously approved. Perhaps the main reason why the match didn't take hold was that Greg's personal compass was pointed to away. He constantly sought out news on "How things were going in the States?" But his plans to emigrate were on hold; Greg had made a promise to his father to stay put until Kevin, with his head full of ideas, could take charge.

While Greg honed his courting skills, Mr. Hadeed and my father would share something cold to drink. They would punctuate their silences with the smallest observations: the weather and the traffic, places where bargains could be found, or the name of a tradesman who still did an honest day's work.

My mother and Mrs. Hadeed knew each other from church. I was close in age to Antonia — one of the in-the-middle Hadeeds, and my sister Marcia was in the same class at school with the youngest Hadeed. The pattern of friendship between our two families was established early on: we went to each other's houses on special occasions, but there was nothing formal about those occasions, and any event on the liturgical calendar was reason enough. In fact, the first memory I have of going to the Hadeeds was after an Easter high mass. (A high mass was an endurance test, in Latin, a spiritual marathon that often ran to more than three sweltering hours. The starch in our Sunday best would start to scratch, and we would be limp and hoarse well before the incense-filled finale.) An invitation from either family was simply a way of making it clear that food was involved.

The Hadeeds' house was on the curve of a hill: the slope from the roadway to their house felt like stepping into the shade of another country under an escort of fig trees and grape vines. Mr. Hadeed had great success with his figs, but his grapes were a story of failure to which he added a new chapter each year. He shaded his trellis with netting carefully placed to hold the morning dew; he planted flowers to attract bees, and shrubs to hold the soil. But conditions were never right for the grapes, and the only consolation he drew from his efforts was that his wife could use the grape leaves in her cooking.

At the end of their long sloping driveway there was a loosely attached *porte-cochère*. The Hadeeds had stopped using their front door entirely; the way into their house and their lives was through the *porte-cochère* and into the kitchen. From the inside you could see how the house had been added to over and again to accommodate a family that had expanded to seven children.

The kitchen was Mrs. Hadeed's domain. If you wandered in there for any reason — a glass of water, a cloth to wipe up a spill — you could be seconded on the spot, and find yourself chopping vegetables or shelling peas: a sudden player in a delicious movement towards some memorable feast. Mrs. Hadeed cooked with an open hand, ingredients came straight from her garden, and were freely substituted into her improvised recipes. Her cooking reflected her upbringing and her marriage: she was a no-nonsense woman who raised and fed seven children, and a husband. Nothing was ever wasted, and every time she cooked, she made more than a little extra for her freezer.

The gallery on the far side of the house was Mr. Hadeed's retreat. He would take his Turkish coffee, his backgammon set, and all the men with him. Mr. Hadeed was soft-spoken in such a way that you had to come close to hear what he had to say. He had the second-language speaker's habit of exaggerating his facial expressions, which was quite disconcerting, and although he was fluent, he often hesitated for an extra second or two before he spoke. This gave his words an extra, almost conspiratorial sort of weight.

Mr. Hadeed made it sound as though he backed into his opportunities, but he was far more shrewd than lucky. His reputation was built on reliability, which was no small feat in a South American country where, as soon as workers were skilled enough, they set up shop on their own or sought to emigrate. Mrs. Hadeed's attentions were focused on the marriage prospects of her five daughters. Only one of her daughters, Yasmin, the eldest, was married. And that marriage was on the rocks.

The breakup of Yasmin's marriage was done in the reverse of her courtship. When her husband came to the house now, he went straight to her old bedroom. He would be allowed some time alone with Stephanie, their only child. He would then beat a retreat past Mr. Hadeed in the gallery and back-pedal through Mrs. Hadeed's kitchen, where he was no longer invited to help. Sometimes he would manage to persuade Yasmin to sit and talk with him in his car. They would roll up all the windows in a futile attempt to stop their arguments from spilling out, but soon the overheated air would be full of recriminations, and Mrs. Hadeed would find some excuse to go out to the *porte-cochère* and show her face, to stop the neighbours from getting a free show.

We liked going to the Hadeeds. Some drama was always in rehearsal, or about to unfold.

Farouk and Faraj Ayoub were half-brothers — same father different mothers. They came to my father for the same sort of business advice that he gave to the Hadeeds, and my father could see how and where they had mutual interests. My mother encouraged the introductions; she saw Farouk and Faraj as potential suitors for the Hadeeds' daughters.

The Ayoubs and Mr. and Mrs. Hadeed were all born in Lebanon,

but to us they were "Syrians." The subtleties and the blunt reali-
ties of Middle East politics escaped us. We painted with a broad
brush: anyone and everyone from the Middle East was "Syrian." At
a time when everyone (except for the odd Englishman in khaki)
still did business in suit and tie, the Ayoubs wore t-shirts and blue
jeans. The Ayoubs brought on a revolution; they went for the
guerrilla strike — take a quick profit and get out — a new hustling
way of doing business.

Farouk and Faraj became backgammon regulars in Mr. Hadeed's
gallery. They had the hugely entertaining habit of rehearsing in
detail key scenes from their business lives. They would script out
what they planned to say to Customs, for example, and act it out
in front of us.

"Mr. Ayoub?" Farouk would take the role of customs officer.
"Why you have all these stereos, man?"

Faraj would shake his head in a wide no as he pretended to
read from an imaginary waybill. "Look at this — this kiss-my-ass
Yankee done gone and send down all these blasted stereos. Box
them up and send them back. By the time I pay the duty —"

"Don't say that!" Farouk interjected. "Don't raise the question
of payment yet."

"Box it up," Faraj resumed. "But they look so nice. Take one
out. Let me see one before *you* send it back."

"That's better," Farouk encouraged, before he returned to
being the stern customs officer.

"It's such a nice unit," Faraj sang its praises. "It could run on
batteries or on a cord. It have AM. It have FM. And it can record
too. It's a shame to send it all the way back to the Yankee? But
what else can I do?"

"Good, good," Farouk coached. "Let him nibble. Now give him
something good to chew."

"Chief," Faraj sighed as he pointed to his imaginary waybill,
"you think anybody could want a stereo system like this?"

"All right," Farouk closed in. "You have him, now reel him in
fast."

"Chief? Could you see yourself with one of these?" Faraj led with trump.

"Chief?" Faraj came a step closer. "Lend me your pen." Faraj scribbled on the imaginary waybill, and then presented it to the customs officer. "Tell me if you think that is a fair number?"

"What would you do if he says no?" Farouk countered.

"I give him back his pen, and ask him to write down his number," Faraj replied.

"Are you offering me a bribe? Mr. Ayoub?" Farouk reverted to his role as the stern customs officer. He wore the indignant long-look of an offended official, and then he would break into a large smile as another plan was hatched.

What the Ayoubs had was contacts, all over the United States, England, and as far away as Australia, in any country with an established pocket of Lebanese. They made money by moving the surplus from one pocket to the next, they lived in the near future, and they were always on the lookout for the next big thing.

Mr. Hadeed reserved judgement on Farouk and Faraj. The bond of coming from the same country still held some currency with Mr. Hadeed, and he understood from personal experience how you have to be aggressive when you are just starting out in business. Mrs. Hadeed promptly dismissed Farouk and Faraj as potential suitors for her unmarried daughters. Those Ayoub boys were a little too old, and a lot too fast. But her still married daughter, Yasmin, added a new scandal to her portfolio when she took up hot and sweaty with the Ayoubs, doing business, and even going abroad on trips with them.

Yasmin, of all the Hadeed children, had the most flair for business. She understood intuitively, like the Ayoubs, what would fly and what you could flip. Yasmin never asked for help from her father, her husband or her two brothers. She always returned from her trips abroad with fresh ideas and a suitcase full of cosmetics that paid her way several times over. She made a business out of anything, and from almost nothing: she turned flowers from the garden into arrangements for weddings and wreaths for funerals; she cut hair and catered, mostly to the whims of those who thought anything foreign and imported was bound to be better than local.

"Those Ayoubs can talk for so," Greg marvelled at the easy theatrical way the Ayoubs could slip into an American or an English accent, as they recounted some recent adventure.

"They have more mouth than money." Kevin was less taken with the Ayoubs, and he resented the effortless way they made money. He felt that the benefits were all too one-sided. It was the Hadeed name that opened doors in the local merchant community and made it possible for the Ayoubs to have such success.

Kevin had pushed for the factory to add new machinery, and he was anxious to see some returns. He repeatedly pressed the Ayoubs to find a deal that would benefit the factory, and when nothing materialized, he was none too subtle in directing his scorn at Yasmin for setting a bad example for her daughter Stephanie, "by gallivanting all over the place with those Ayoubs."

Yasmin enjoyed being the centre of a scandal, and Kevin's scorn sounded more like envy to her. She had a big sister's knowledge and years of practice at getting under his skin. Yasmin in turn belittled Kevin for his "failure to understand the past or to see the future that's staring you in the face."

Whenever our families got together, Kevin was always the first one to leave, one huff short of a full-blown argument. My father seldom commented publicly or privately about the personal or business dealings of any of his clients, but he did remark more than once, that if Yasmin, the eldest Hadeed child, had been born male, a different and perhaps more natural order of succession surely would have prevailed.

Farouk and Faraj provided more than colour commentary at the fierce backgammon matches in Mr. Hadeed's gallery; they also gave "breaking news on all fronts" about "the situation in Lebanon." The Ayoubs were not at all concerned with who was winning and who was losing. They expressed no religious commitment or preference for either side. They viewed the war in

terms of shortages and windfalls, and debated the logistical chal-
lenges of matching supply with demand.

Like many expatriates, Mr. Hadeed retained a keen interest in
the politics of his homeland. He admitted "to being a hot-head in
his day," and those passions had directly contributed to his leaving. His parents had arranged a quick marriage and a fresh start
for him and his new bride, "far away from all the madness that is
still going on."

Mr. Hadeed had no regrets about leaving the writing of history
to others. He had never been back to Lebanon. He cited business
pressures and family commitments, and over the years his com-
munication with his past had dwindled to infrequent and formal
letters: the sort of letters that had taken weeks or even months to
arrive, and were most likely to be of events already concluded and
only for the official record. But now whenever Mr. Hadeed won-
dered aloud about whatever became of so and so? the Ayoubs with
their network of connections could provide him with detailed updates in hours if not minutes.

Perhaps it was all this reminiscing with the Ayoubs that brought
the idea of returning to Lebanon to the forefront. Or perhaps it
was as obvious as an old man looking to close the long circle of his
life. Mr. Hadeed began to plan a pilgrimage. Initially Mrs. Hadeed
was reluctant to go with him; she had been back three times over
the years, and she still retained enough of the taste of what it's
like. She measured time and place like so many mothers, by the
respective ages of her children. Her first trip back to Lebanon was
"when Yasmin was eleven, Greg was nine and Antonia was four."

On that first trip back, Mrs. Hadeed stayed for nearly a year.
Yasmin and Antonia went with her. Yasmin became completely
fluent in Arabic, an accomplishment that is still pointed to by Mrs.
Hadeed. Kevin holds the distinction of being the only one of her
children who was born in Lebanon. Greg, who was left behind
with his father, still makes a joke with a serious face about "being
abandoned."

Mrs. Hadeed's second and third trips were both for funerals.

First her father, then her mother. Yasmin was by then "big enough to see about the others," and Mrs. Hadeed made those passages alone.

The planning of Mr. Hadeed's trip was the subject of many swirling conversations in the kitchen and gallery and around the dinner table. Mrs. Hadeed allowed herself to be persuaded after Yasmin agreed to let her take Stephanie along. Stephanie, the only grand-child so far, had a Shirley Temple–like existence at the centre of her grandparents' attentions. And the winning argument was that "with her brains, Stephanie was sure to pick up Arabic in two-twos."

The Ayoubs provided the clinching reason; they brokered a deal that involved a shipment of parts from the Hadeeds' factory to Lebanon. The trip was now official — a legitimate business expense. And, the Ayoubs boasted, they already had a third party lined up, whose share of the expenses would pay for the entire trip. All Mr. Hadeed had to do was to go and enjoy himself.

We lived in a place too small for secrets, and Greg was all mouth. Even when the joke was at his expense, Greg was willing to pay the price for a good story. When he was dating my aunt Lydia, we saw a bit of his serious side, and he confirmed some of the old gossip that got passed around about his family.

"Dad used to take me to work with him on Saturdays," Greg recalled. "Mammy insisted that he take one child out from under her feet for a few hours.

"When business was good, the factory would run an extra shift on Saturdays. The workers would grumble but they were glad for the extra money, and went about their jobs with a sense of purpose that made my dad smile. But most Saturdays were filled with the drudgery of running a business. Dad would bury himself in paperwork, and I would play some version of hide-and-seek among the machinery or out in the storage yard.

"On the way home, Dad made a regular stop at a shantytown

about half a mile from the factory. 'I won't be long, you stay here in the car.' Dad always gave me a direct order. But after a few minutes I would get out and go over to a standpipe on the main road. There were always a few children playing in the water that they were sent to fetch, and I would join them.

"I had just turned nine. It was one of those Saturdays, and in that part of the afternoon when the sun goes from bake to broil. I decided to follow my new playmates from the standpipe back to the shantytown. I was about to return to the car when I heard my dad's voice and I went by reflex towards it.

"Dad was speaking in Arabic," Greg said. "He only did that when he was very angry or very excited. Dad was inside one of the shacks. At first I couldn't make him out through the cracks. He was lying flat on his back, and he was almost completely blocked from view by a woman who had her hair in short braids which were sticking out at all angles.

"As my eyes adjusted to the shade, I saw two big circles on her chest and a dark triangle between her legs. She settled the suspicions that I had about the way things really were. She climbed on and began to ride my dad.

"I raced back to the car, giddy and full of secrets. And then I felt a sharp sensation. I had stepped on a nail and it went deep into the fleshy ball of my foot. I could see it sticking out between my second and third toes. Some instinct made me elevate my foot, but I couldn't stand to draw the nail out by myself. And there was no way that I was going to hobble back to the shack.

"By the time Dad found me, my foot had swollen to twice its normal size. Dad immediately cried out for help. After a short debate it was decided to remove the nail first, and then go to the hospital for a tetanus shot. The woman from the shack tried to hold me tight against her sweaty body so Dad could draw out the nail, but I twisted and fought with all fury against her."

"Be still," Dad said. "Be a man."

A few days later, Greg's mother and his two sisters left for Lebanon. And a wounded Greg was the only one left behind, with his father, to be a man.

⌒

The time finally came for Mr. Hadeed to embark on his pilgrimage. Yasmin drove her parents and Stephanie to the airport. It was not the first time for Stephanie to fly, but Yasmin felt that this would be the first trip that Stephanie would be able to remember.

The first time Yasmin got on a plane she was eleven. From the minute she was airborne, she knew that her life had changed forever. There were no direct flights to Lebanon in those days; the connections are still difficult, but back then it was an epic journey. During the flight her little sister Antonia erupted or secreted something from every hole in her body, and Yasmin had to look after her the entire flight. Her mother cried an ocean of tears all the while sticking to the fiction that she was crying because she was afraid of flying. But Yasmin had decoded the real reason; her parents had had a huge fight. They did their best arguing in Arabic, and Yasmin could make fair to good guesses about most of what they said. Yasmin told her mother that she knew all about everything. She knew what her father had done, and she knew all about love. This made her mother cry all the more.

Mrs. Hadeed had accepted the hurried match made for her by her family. It was a time when nothing was certain, and everybody was looking for a way out of Lebanon. There was a boy whom she secretly cared about, but she chose not to speak up. She abandoned love. And all that came and went with it.

"So Yasmin?" her mother asked. "You already know everything there is to know about love?" Yasmin shook her head with all of her eleven years' worth of certainty in her seat high above the clouds. And then she parroted something else that she must have overheard, "It only hurts for a little while, and then, it's all gone."

⌒

Mr. Hadeed sighed as he braced for takeoff; he'd never felt comfortable with the speed of airplanes — a smaller world is not a better world. His wife held his hand, and he squeezed hers tight. Mrs. Hadeed was under no illusions that her wistful husband was wishing for a second honeymoon. She was extra glad to have Stephanie along; she filled in the silences between them. Mrs. Hadeed had her own mission to complete, for she was most determined to find good matches for her unmarried daughters. You cannot leave something like that to love. She had let Yasmin have a try with love, and look how that turned out? On her first trip back to Lebanon, she herself had sought out love. She went back to see the boy who remained in her heart. But she couldn't find the boy in the man he had become, and she began to doubt if love was ever really there. One thing is for certain, she knew. It doesn't just hurt for a little while and then is all gone . . . What remains is like some lumpy thing unborn.

After an absence of nearly a year, Mrs. Hadeed returned from that first trip to Lebanon, back to her husband.

"How are things?" Mr. Hadeed had had a year to think about his marriage.

"Things are hopeful," his wife said. "Everybody is speaking the language of peace."

"Perhaps this time," her husband said, "things will work out?" Mr. Hadeed was glad to have his wife and children back. He was surprised to learn that he had a brand new son. Kevin was a good name, he agreed. He had a surprise for her as well, look, he had built a trellis, and he had planted some grapevines . . .

An impatient Kevin was down at the factory waiting on the Ayoubs. The profits from this deal would prove to his father and Greg that he could run things on his own. He knew how much Greg wanted out, and now he had no reason to stay. Those blasted Ayoubs, Kevin fumed. They had pestered him constantly for their share. As soon as Greg confirmed that the payment for the shipment had arrived, he had called them. And now they were late. Let those blasted Ayoubs make all the style they want; if they want to play games, he can make them wait too. They won't see a cent now, until he is good and ready. He's going home to his wife and his supper.

About a half mile away from the factory, where the road crosses the shantytown, the police arrested Kevin. And that was when my father was called. Two sets of his clients were involved.

"The ones you really have to watch out for are those who don't believe in anything." That was all my father — in his usual elliptical way — had to say. Greed, of course, was their undoing: the third party that the Ayoubs had found to stick with all the shipping costs were arms smugglers. The Ayoubs disavowed all knowledge, but no one bought their claims of innocence. And it cost them in other ways; the local merchant community refused to have any further dealings with them. They were out on bail when they took off on a business trip from which they never returned.

My father never said so directly, but he felt that the Hadeeds must have also known from the start that they were involved with something. Kevin put the blame squarely on the Ayoubs for everything; he was tied up in so many legal proceedings that Yasmin had to jump in and take charge of the factory. It never came out how the authorities were alerted to the scheme. The shipment was let through so arrests could be made on both sides. Mr. Hadeed was detained in Lebanon for interrogation, but he was released when it was discovered that there were no illegal arms components in the shipment from his factory after all. No one knew how or what had happened; the arms components had simply disappeared.

Greg had also disappeared. He got clean away with all the money. For the longest while no one knew where Greg was or what became of him. Then my aunt Lydia, whom he had dated for a time, received a card from him. He was somewhere "in the States." He had "the fondest memories" and offered his "best wishes," but that was all it said.

It wasn't all that long after his big trip to Lebanon that Mr. Hadeed took ill. And although it wasn't all that sudden, it was still a surprise when he died. By then I was doing the very thing that I swore I'd never do — join my father's firm to do exactly the kind of soliciting that I had always poked fun at — wills and probate. I felt like some sort of low priest, transferring through paperwork the store of one generation to the next. I saw a lot of the Hadeeds right after Mr. Hadeed died, and I broke one of the cardinal rules: I dated a client's daughter.

Antonia is my age. We practically grew up together, and the only wonder was why it took us so long. "Sometimes you can't see the very thing that is right in front of you," Mrs. Hadeed said. Everyone approved.

It would've been more accurate to say that Antonia and I were "staying in" than "going out." The perils of the world had washed up in our backwater; everyone had a horror story to relate. Robbery and rape had become so commonplace that even the simplest excursion could end in abject terror. We countered by travelling in convoys, and dating became a military-style group exercise.

The Hadeed household, with a handful of unmarried women, became a church of a different kind. It was the place to be socially, the *porte-cochère* was converted into a staging area where suitors awaiting entry could discuss the events of the day. The readymade excuse of business to attend and my longstanding connection to the Hadeed family got me into the express line. After that, like everyone else, I had to get past Yasmin.

Even before Mr. Hadeed died, Yasmin had become the de facto head of the household. All prospective suitors had to pass her screening, and she determined who advanced from the *porte-cochère* to the gallery, and who received the coveted invitations to stay for dinner. Some things remained the same: you were truly in when you were asked to help out in the kitchen.

Yasmin also dictated the sleeping-over arrangements. Sleepingover did not mean sex. Among the unmarried, sex was logistically a near impossibility. It meant extended furtive foreplay, and a night alone on a narrow cot in the gallery where you could let your ardour cool under a blanket of stars. Sleeping-over meant that you had strayed beyond the ridiculously early governmentimposed curfew, or that you had missed your convoy. It became a clear rule: never travel alone, never travel unless there are at least three cars going together. The protocols for this new order were actually determined by newcomers; there had been an influx of young men from Lebanon in recent years. They had grown up in a climate of civil war, and they would have chillingly normal conversations about the best ways to run a police roadblock, or what to say or not say while being interrogated. Our local level of unrest was commonplace to them; they already knew what to expect and what was expected, and so we took our cues from them.

The opening topic of every conversation now was "Canada or the States?" My sister Marcia went from studying in Canada to marrying a Canadian and starting a family. My mother took frequent and extended trips to Canada to supervise. The workload at my father's firm shifted from wills and probate to offshore tax shelters and exit visas.

"Everyone is leaving; the life we had is gone," my father said. And he often repeated his dry observation that if I wanted to keep working, I would have to follow suit and jump ship with our clients.

These were the conditions and circumstances under which Antonia and I began dating; sex was an occasion that we had to plot and plan for, sometimes weeks ahead. Antonia would lay the groundwork. She would begin by having migraines, by establishing the pre-existence of migraines, so that when the opportunity arose, her excuse would be ready-set.

The best opportunities were on Sundays. We circled those Sundays with a high mass on our calendar. Mrs. Hadeed never missed a high mass, and Yasmin always escorted her. A high mass meant several uninterrupted hours. It was great, great sex. And then, Mrs. Hadeed died.

Yasmin tried to maintain the status quo, but Antonia refused to put up with it any longer. She was a fully grown woman, and she would no longer be treated like a child.

"Don't be such a fool." Big sister Yasmin always knew the quickest way to get under the skin of any of her siblings. "No man will buy the cow if he can get the milk for free."

"You sound just like Mammy," was all Antonia could counter with.

"You just watch," Yasmin planted the worm. "You'll see."

Perhaps under other circumstances our relationship would have run a different course, but I think we would have come out at the same place. We tried and tried, but we couldn't recapture the intensity of our passion. We attempted to recreate the patterns that had been so stimulating for us. We abstained all week, hoping to get our Sundays back. We tried my place, but when it was broken into and vandalized, we agreed with relief that it was not safe at all, and perhaps it would be best if we went back to the way it was. But we couldn't go back, and even worse, we couldn't agree on a future. I had come to the same conclusion as my father; it was time to join the exodus. Antonia was still determined to wait and see. For weeks we had the same awkward rewinding conversation in the driveway outside the Hadeed house, until it seemed like we were talking about two other people.

Mrs. Hadeed had left her affairs in good order. My father's firm handled the probate, her will was settled quickly, and there was no shortage of legitimate excuses: I stopped going to the Hadeeds.

About a year after Mrs. Hadeed died, I received a call from Yasmin. She was having a requiem mass said, and I was invited back to the house afterwards. Yasmin's invitation was an olive branch, and the meal was going to be extra special.

"It's taken us a year," Yasmin said, "but we've finally reached the bottom of Mammy's freezer — it's the very last bit of Mammy's cooking."

The requiem mass was packed. Weddings and funerals were practically the only public gatherings still allowed. And people attended for the chance to have a social outing, and to see who else was still around. My intention was to pay my respects and beg off. But Yasmin would have none of that; she sent Kevin over to make it clear that I was expected back at the house.

Kevin had gone from short to stout in a hurry. His wife was very pregnant, and he was eating to keep pace with her.

"She could drop it right here in church." Kevin was a very expectant father.

"You would have no choice but to name the baby after a saint in such a circumstance," I said.

"The government is planning to nationalize me," Kevin confided.

I had heard about that, and it was more than just rumour. Kevin, always so intent on being his own boss, was now faced with having to answer to a whole lot of bosses.

"We can't talk business in church. Come back to the house," Kevin whispered. He had always liked his intrigue.

"How is your father these days?" Yasmin asked.

"He's supposed to be easing into retirement," I said. "But he's busier than ever. A lot of people are voting with their feet and taking their wallets with them. He and Mom are in Canada; Marcia is manufacturing another grandchild. He sends his regrets."

"Well it's too bad your father is not here," Yasmin said. "He loved Mammy's cooking."

"Her stuffed eggplant is his all-time favourite," I agreed. "My mom tried to make it, but it never came out the same. She always accused your mother of withholding some secret ingredient."

"I watched her make it so many times," Yasmin said, "but I can never get it right. The only one who can cook like Mammy is Antonia."

Antonia's lips are sealed. She's not going to give up the secret either. One of the young men in the gallery is her new suitor, but I'm not sure which one.

"The future does come so quick, and I have Stephanie to think about." Yasmin had new business on her agenda.

"Greg is already fixed-up. Things are organized on his side." Kevin revealed the direction of their plan. "We're looking to bail out in an orderly fashion."

"I have my parachute packed too," I assured them. And I recited the standard checklist. "Don't tell anybody that you're leaving. Don't put your house up for sale yet. Sell your cars and lease instead. When the first buyout offer comes from the government, scream like bloody hell about how insulted you are."

For once, Yasmin and Kevin were in total agreement. Antonia listened intently to the plan taking shape, but didn't say a word. She took the dish of stuffed eggplants out of the oven and peeked under the tinfoil to see how it was coming along. Antonia exited through the *porte-cochère* and into the garden. Yasmin asked me to stay and help out in the kitchen.

"Antonia says she's not leaving this house," Yasmin revealed another worry. "You try and talk some sense into her. She listens to you."

"I don't know about that," I said. "We both know how hard it is to get Antonia to change once her mind is set."

Outside, Mrs. Hadeed's garden was a riot of abundance, and Mr. Hadeed's grapevines were finally having a bumper year. His trellis was deeply bowed by the weight of all those grapes. Antonia was working on a support for the base of the trellis.

"Your dad would be astonished by all these grapes," I said. "What did you do so different?"

"Sometimes it's best just to leave things alone." Antonia took a step back to inspect her repairs. The trellis still had an uncertain tilt to it.

"It's going to need more than a brace," I suggested.

"You don't think it's worth fixing?" Antonia asked.

"Things can reach a point where it's best to just start over," I said.

"I thought you'd be long gone by now."

"There's more to do than I expected, but all the loose ends are just about tied off now," I said. "Yasmin is worried about you."

"I won't agree to sell the house. That's what she's so worried about. Did she send you to give some legal reason why I must do whatever she wants?"

"No," I said. "I'm talking to you as a friend. You can't stay here. Everyone is leaving. What's left?"

Antonia resumed work on the base of the trellis with all seriousness. She dug her fingers deep into the soil. It felt as if I were standing watch over her.

We could hear Yasmin yelling at the top of her lungs for everyone to come and eat.

"It's time to go in." I offered to help Antonia up but she turned away from me. She was crying.

"I remember when Daddy came back from his big trip to Lebanon," Antonia said. "He told us he never should have left Lebanon in the first place. He said he should have stayed and faced his destiny."

"What did your mother have to say about that?" I asked.

"'Don't talk such nonsense! Do the best with what you have!'" Antonia gave the exact citation from her mother's big book of no-nonsense sayings.

I offered her my hand again, and this time she accepted. I pulled her to her feet, and we started towards the house. After a moment Antonia stopped to fix her face. She took a good long look around her mother's garden and said, "I really don't know how Mammy kept everything growing so well for so long."

ABOUT THE AUTHOR

F.B. André was born in San Fernando, Trinidad, in 1955. After immigrating to Canada in
1971, he worked at diverse jobs — in factories,
in mining, in catering, as a program adminis-
trator, a café owner, and teacher. All of these
experiences inform and enrich his writing.
His stories have been published in several
magazines and anthologies. His first collection
of short stories *The Man Who Beat the Man* was published by
NeWest Press. He lives in Vancouver.

MEMBER OF SCABRINI GROUP

Québec, Canada
2007